DISAPPEARANCE: A PREMONITIONS MYSTERY

by Jude Watson

SCHOLASTIC INC.
New York   Toronto   London   Auckland   Sydney
Mexico City   New Delhi   Hong Kong   Buenos Aires

For Ric
rest in peace, baby

No part of this publication may be reproduced, stored in a retrieval system, or transmitted in any form or by any means, electronic, mechanical, photocopying, recording, or otherwise, without written permission of the publisher. For information regarding permission, write to Scholastic Inc., Attention: Permissions Department, 557 Broadway, New York, NY 10012.

All rights reserved. Published by Scholastic Inc. SCHOLASTIC and associated logos are trademarks and/or registered trademarks of Scholastic Inc.

ISBN 0-439-69688-7

12 11 10 9 8 7 6 5 4 3 2 1   5 6 7 8 9 10/0

Printed in the U.S.A.   01

First printing, August 2005

When she hands me my change,
I feel a pain that lives inside her,
a restlessness that won't go away.
Two days later, Susan Reilly abandons
her husband and children and runs away
to Las Vegas. For good.

When he takes my spaghetti order, I know
the waiter is worried that his wife is
cheating on him.
She is.

I can feel what people want . . . and
what they're willing to do to get it.

What if you could feel what other people
felt . . . and it was unbearable?

What if you saw what was going to
happen . . . and you couldn't stop it?
What if that something was murder?

ONE

I should have known that Saturday afternoon would turn out to be a disaster. And believe me, when I say I should have known, *I should have known.*

It all begins with a girl called Marigold. She's the inexplicable love object of my cousin Diego. I guess her gorgeousness makes up for a certain lack of charisma. For Diego, that is. For the rest of us, we just have to deal with trying to make conversation with someone with the personality of plankton. Diego has dated just about every pretty girl on the island of Beewick, and he's made inroads onto the mainland, even as far as Seattle. But Marigold, for some reason, knocked him stupid.

Well, she *is* a knockout, in that long-blond-hair, long-legged, blue-eyed category that makes other girls want to either be her best friend or poison her caffeine-free chai.

So when Diego asks me that Saturday afternoon in November if I want to hang with them and Marigold's brother, I should say no, considering that Marigold's conversation sends me into a coma and I consider her brother about as appetizing as brussels sprouts.

I look at Diego and Marigold for a minute while I make up my mind. I know I should be concentrating on answering, but I'm thinking about how beautiful people just naturally click together, like magnets. Maybe it's just as simple as that. Diego is tall and lean and so handsome that once I saw a waitress drop an entire tray of glasses when he walked into a restaurant.

Marigold is leaning against Diego, and she has a hand in the back pocket of his jeans. It's another thing that bugs me about her. She's always leaning against him, as though she can't stand up by herself.

Marigold flashes her halogen smile. "Come on, Gracie. This is Washington State. You've got to grab the sunshine while you can."

You see? Pick the most obvious thing, and she'll say it.

"Yeah," Diego says. "Pretty soon it will be January and the sun will be on semipermanent hiatus."

Marigold laughs as if that's the funniest thing she's ever heard.

"Okay," I say.

Well, what else was I going to do? Homework?

We take off in Diego's old VW, the one he bought with his landscaping money from the summer. The windows are open, because it's such an amazing day, so I can't hear the conversation in the front seat. Which is good, because Marigold is talking. The hum of tires on the road is far more riveting.

So I look at the scenery, which is not exactly a hardship. I moved from Maryland to the Pacific Northwest only last year, after my mother was killed in a car crash. My aunt Shay took me in. Now I live on an island off the coast of Washington State, in Puget Sound.

I hated Beewick Island when I first got here. It was February, and February is not the best month here. There's a permanent drizzle, and it's cold, yet you don't get the benefits of snow. But after about nine months here, I realize why, when you ask a Pacific Northwesterner the best thing about living here, they say "the weather." It's no joke. It's just our secret, that if you can get past the winter rain, the rest of the year is not too hot, not too cold. You can practically live outside.

Beewick is about an hour north of Seattle, if you drive really fast. The island is almost a hundred miles long but only a few miles wide, with wicked cliffs on the north end and gentle farmland on the south. The sky seems higher here, and bluer. Off to the west are the snowcapped Olympic Mountains. Sometimes they just seem like clouds on the horizon, and then on clear days they startle you with their presence. The Sound is the color of blueberries, and there are fields of farmland and lavender. It's a pretty nice place to live, and it is a tribute to my stubbornness that it took me close to six months to admit it.

We drive into Greystone Harbor, the closest town to us, and Diego pulls into a space outside the Harborside restaurant.

"We're going here?" I ask.

"They have the best fried clams," Marigold says.

Maybe he won't be here. Maybe it's his day off. But I see Zed's faded red Subaru parked in the lot, and I know he's here. It's hard facing the person you put in jail for kidnapping when he didn't do a thing. It really is.

Last summer, my friend Emily disappeared. I'd had a vision, and it had seemed to connect to Zed. By the time I'd figured out that the kidnapper wasn't Zed, the police had nailed him for tackling me and demanding why, exactly, I was going around saying he was guilty.

Oops is not up there on a list of acceptable apologies for this.

The thing I can't admit, hardly even to myself, is that I still think about the moment he tackled me and we rolled down the hill, how his chest felt so solid, how his breath felt against my skin. I was terrified at the time, but now I can look back and dissect every detail. Which I do. Frequently.

I am *so* glad there isn't another me around to see my thoughts.

I tag after Diego and Marigold into the

restaurant. Marigold's twin brother, Mason, is already here with a table full of his friends. They're all jocks, on the swimming team and the soccer team, and most of them aren't too awful. I just feel like I'm disappearing when I'm around them. I'm not the kind of girl they notice. I'm short, and I have brown hair and brown eyes and a devotion to gray sweaters. Not exactly a head turner.

Zed is waiting tables, and he looks up and sees me. This would be a lot easier if he weren't so good-looking. He has silvery-gray eyes and black hair he cut short over the summer. He looks startled to see me, as if he can't believe I have the nerve to show up in his father's place. Zed works here and in Seattle, at a glassblower's studio. We've seen each other since that whole thing last summer, of course — we live only a mile from Greystone Harbor, and it's a small town — but we've always managed to just nod at each other and look away.

Mason yells at us to hurry up, he wants to order, and Marigold and Diego head over.

"Hey, everybody, you know Gracie, Diego's cousin," Marigold says. "Gracie, everyone." The guys all look at me and say "hey," or slurp their sodas.

Marigold sits down on an empty chair next to Mason. Diego sits next to her. The only other chair is at the other end of the table, next to Dylan Brewer, one of Mason's friends. I go and sit there.

This is going to be fun, I can just feel it. All the thrills of a filling without novocaine.

They immediately launch into a discussion of some college football game that's going to be on tomorrow afternoon. That doesn't stop them from dissecting what is going to happen and who is going to totally rock.

It makes you think. Here I am, somebody who can occasionally see things that are going to happen. But when it comes to who's going to win a football game or have the winning lottery number, I'm totally useless.

I watch as Marigold takes a sip of her diet soda and offers the straw to Diego. Everyone orders fried clams, including me, even though I'm not crazy about fried clams. But I can't quite meet Zed's eyes when he takes the order. Still, he hesitates next to me. I stare at the silver ring he wears on his thumb.

"So, how've you been?" he says.

I look up. I feel ice crack and the earth turn. I realize, at that very moment, at long last, that Zed does not hold a grudge. Relief washes through me.

"Okay," I say.

"Good."

This dazzling display of conversational skill ends when Zed nods a good-bye. He tucks the order pad into the back waistband of his pants, which in my addled state I find an incredibly cool move. Then he heads into the kitchen.

The platters of food arrive quickly, which I'm happy about, because I haven't been able to think of a single thing to say while we were waiting. Nobody noticed, though. Mason and his friends have moved on from football to soccer. These kinds of guys can only talk about sports. I think it's a kind of primitive form of communication for guys, like gorillas making hand signals. Diego and Marigold are having an intense conversation by themselves. It looks like they could be arguing, but I try not to feel hopeful about the possibility.

I eat a couple of clams dunked in lots of cocktail sauce, and most of my fries, while sneaking glances at Zed waiting on tables. Occasionally, he'll smile at a customer, and it's worth waiting for.

Then Mason's friends start making fun of a couple at the next table. They're eating the Greystone oysters that Beewick Island is known for and looking out at the blue sweep of bay, and you can take one look at them and know they're from Seattle. Not that there's anything wrong with Seattle. But they look pretty rich and they're wearing pressed khakis and cashmere sweaters that are pretending to be sweatshirts, and Mason starts to goof on them.

"I'll have the plucky little Chardonnay, muffin, how about you?" he says.

Totally lame, but his buddies all guffaw.

Mason and his friends are the kind of goons

who think that because they're lucky enough to have lived all their lives on a beautiful island in Puget Sound they get to make fun of the week-enders. It's true that real estate prices have been zooming lately, and that more and more land is being gobbled up for development. But I don't think this couple from Seattle, out to have a nice seafood lunch on a Saturday, deserves to get heck-led for it.

Meanwhile, Marigold is feeding Diego a French fry. I guess they made up.

I don't think the couple heard what Mason said, but somehow they know the snickers rolling across the room are directed at them. Zed turns, and I see his face darken. He strides over to our table. I wonder if I can assume the molecular struc-ture of a chair and disappear completely. Zed thinks I'm friends with these cretins.

He rips the check off his pad.

"Whoa, dude," Mason says. "You didn't ask about dessert."

"You want dessert?" Zed asks. "There's a great ice cream parlor across the street. Our pies suck." He drops the check on the table and walks away.

"Whoa," Mason says. "Touchy Waiter Boy thinks we're rude."

"Yeah, you're upsetting the clientele, Patterson," Dylan says. Mason and his friends usually call each other by their last names, which is kind of funny because most of them have last names for first names anyway.

Andy Hassam pushes away his plate. "We should push their cars off the ferry, man. All we get from them is traffic and garbage. Pretty soon we won't be able to eat our own oysters. The water will be too polluted."

Everyone knows why Andy hates the weekenders and the new summer people. His family owns a farm. Last year they had to sell a chunk of their land to a developer, who built a whole bunch of houses on the site. Nobody is happy about it. Hassam's farm stand is a local institution. They have hayrides in the fall and a pumpkin field. Now, instead of overlooking fields of farmland and meadows, it's going to overlook a bunch of BMWs.

"What are you talking about? You don't even like oysters, man. You call them snot on a shell," Dylan says, hooting at Andy.

Andy flushes red. "And what are you talking about, Brewer? You've only lived on Beewick for five minutes."

"Try four years, dude," Dylan shoots back.

"Try all my life, dudette," Andy says.

"I didn't know this was a contest."

Mason's eyes gleam. "Whoa. Do you two need to take this outside?"

"Knock it off, Patterson," Andy mumbles.

"No, I mean *really* outside," Mason says. "On

the deck. Speaking of contests, I have a way to prove who's a true Beewick Islander."

Dylan looks intrigued, but Andy looks like he wants to go home and bond with his Game Cube. Marigold and Diego finally look up from their deep and boring conversation to notice what's going on around them.

"If you're really an islander, you know the tides," Mason says. "You should be able to gauge whether you can dive off the deck safely or not."

Andy looks green. "Dive off the deck?"

"Hey, Mason," Diego says. "Not such a great idea, dude."

"I think it's awesome," Brewer says. "My brother told me that guys used to dive off the decks of all the restaurants on this strip every Groundhog Day."

"It was extreme radical stuff," Mason says. "They called it The Gauntlet. You had to dive off at least three to be a member of the club."

"And they stopped doing it because it was too dangerous," Diego points out. "Somebody broke his leg."

"Which is, like, my point," Mason says. "If you're a real islander, you can figure out if you can do it by watching the water."

"Listen to Diego, Mason," Marigold says.

If Mason had been half-fooling before, now he's committed. You don't have to be psychic to see that he isn't about to let his sister's boyfriend tell him what to do.

"Let's go, dudes," Mason says, pushing back his chair.

Dylan stands up, and Andy has no choice. Diego shakes his head.

I look around for Zed, but he must be in the kitchen. By the time I turn around again, Mason, Dylan, and Andy are outside on the deck, and Dylan is kicking off his shoes.

Suddenly, the room whites out.

Water foaming, arms thrashing . . .

Panic. Fear. A heart bursting, everything bursting. Everything is red now and through the red I see a body falling through murky water.

When I return to where I am, I see that Dylan is looking over the railing. Diego is trying to talk to him. He puts a hand on his arm, but Dylan shakes it off.

I stand up so quickly, I knock my chair over. Across the room, Zed looks over.

"Zed!" I call. "You have to stop him!"

Zed looks out the window to the deck. He slams the tray onto the nearest table and starts to sprint across the dining room. The couple from Seattle look up from their wine.

I run behind Zed, but we're too late. Before we can get there, Dylan hoists himself up on the deck rail, balances for a split second, and dives. Diego shouts, and Mason laughs, and Marigold screams.

We all race to the railing and look over. I can see a white shape under the water, but then it's gone. Ripples are absorbed into the current. It was like Dylan was never even there.

"Diego," I whisper.

"Call 9-1-1," Diego tells Zed.

"Just wait a second," Mason says. "Brewer's laughing at us, man. He'll come up. He's on the swim team."

Diego gives Mason a look that says you-are-the-biggest-idiot-in-the-known-universe, but Mason doesn't see it.

"Come *up,* Dylan!" Marigold shouts.

And then Dylan shoots out of the water, screaming. His eyes are wild, and he strokes toward the beach, shouting. A wash of water hits him in the face, and he chokes.

At first we can't make it out. And then when we hear it, we can't believe what we hear.

"There's a body down there!"

TWO

"I touched it. I touched it."

Dylan sits shivering under a blanket Zed brought out from the restaurant. The police cars are parked in crazy angles on the street. A bunch of officers are talking behind the yellow POLICE LINE DO NOT CROSS tape. Dylan looks as gray as the water. Clouds have formed, blocking the sun, and the wind has picked up. Mason and his friends sit with him, but they don't know what to say for once. Every now and then, one of them mumbles, "Hang in there, dude."

The police divers are just beginning to search when a dark-blue sedan pulls into the Harborside parking lot. Joe Fusilli gets out. I am glad to see him. Joe is a police detective, and he dates my aunt Shay, and I totally believe he will make sense of this situation and demonstrate to Dylan that he touched an old beach ball, or a sunken buoy, not a dead body.

Because I don't want to remember the vision I saw.

Because now I know the vision hadn't been of Dylan Brewer. Deep inside, I know I saw the drowning of that poor body in the bay.

I know it's a man.

I know he fought to live. I know he fought very hard.

Joe looks annoyed to see that we're there. He raises his eyebrows at me for a hello and goes to talk to the police officers.

"Maybe we should leave," Diego says.

"Yeah," I say. We don't move.

I would have thought Marigold would go into hysterics — she definitely seems like a hysterics sort of girl — but she hasn't said much, just looked out at the bay and huddled close to Diego.

"Are you okay?" Diego asks her in a low voice.

She looks up at him and nods bravely, like she was the one who found the body.

A small crowd has gathered in the parking lot. In a small town, word travels fast.

Mason appoints himself the official spokesman. He fills in the passing pedestrians and the waiters from the Crab Shack next door, gradually adding more disgusting details about how the body felt when Dylan's foot hit it.

Most of the people have somewhere to get to and leave after a few minutes, but Joy Elliott, our town librarian, is hanging right in there, watching the cops and the divers in the water. It's clear that dead bodies don't spook her.

Franklin and Jefferson Ferris walk up. They are father and son and own Founders Realty in

Greystone Harbor. Franklin Ferris is about a hundred years old. He's wearing a suit, even though it's Saturday. Jeff is about Shay's age, and he looks like a Before picture of his dad, except in casual mode, wearing a tweed jacket and khakis. I think both Ferrises have an extreme case of If Only We Were Brits.

Joy sees them and jerks her head around, and Jeff makes the same maneuver, swiveling his head and looking straight at us, as if she isn't there. I remember that they dated for a while, and now they can't stand being around each other. Sometimes small towns can get really, really small.

"Look, son," Franklin says. "Ten of our fair town's citizens. Must be a parade."

"Hey, Dylan. Hey, Mason. Whatssup?" Jeff Ferris is one of those adults who thinks using slang is going to make us like them.

Mason fills him in on the police action. "Hey, coach," he says. Jeff also coaches part-time at Beewick High. "Dylan here did an awesome dive; you would have been proud. Except that he bumped into a dead body."

Jeff looks a little green. "Dead body?" He must be thinking how it will impact his real estate business. Diego and I joke about Jeff all the time, because he lives for his work. Every time he sees us, he says, "How's the house doing?" as though Shay's house is a person. He sold it to her when she first came to Beewick about twenty years ago. We always say, "Still standing," just like Shay does.

"A floater," Joy says. She pushes her red glasses up her nose as she looks out at the bay, watching the divers. "Even though it's not floating. That's what the police call a drowned body."

"Charming," Jeff says. "Thanks."

Joy's neck flushes red.

"What an excellent way to begin lunch," Franklin Ferris says. "Come on, Jeff. A dozen Greystones are waiting."

Jeff swallows, as if the thought of oysters at the moment is just about the most unappetizing thing he could imagine. I have to say I agree.

The Ferrises head into the Harborside, Jeff sneaking looks at the bay. Joy looks at her watch and heads off reluctantly.

Marigold shivers. "Imagine eating lunch while they drag the harbor for a body."

"They're not dragging it," I say. "They know where it is. And we were eating lunch while it was down there."

"We don't need the details, Gracie," Diego says to me.

The divers surface for the third time. There's a flurry of activity among the cops. They talk into radios. They walk from one group to another. Joe goes to his car and comes back again.

It seems to take forever, but Joe finally walks over to us.

"You kids should take off," he says.

"That's okay," Mason says. "We —"

Joe hits him with one of his level gazes. Joe isn't a handsome guy, although Shay probably thinks so. He has a thin, drawn face and a big nose, and he looks as though he might sleep two hours a night, if he's lucky. But he does have one terrific pair of brown eyes. They can warm you or slice you up like provolone. He used to be a detective in Seattle, and he's got a certain big-city coolness about him, like he's seen just about everything there is to see.

"You kids should take off," he says again. He looks down at Dylan. "Did you call your parents?"

Dylan is too freaked to even mind that he needs his parents called. He nods. "My dad is picking me up. Was it . . . was it . . ."

"It was a body," Joe says. He takes in Dylan's look of panic. "The first time is hard," he says to Dylan. It's the right approach, like Dylan is a cop, too. "I puked."

"You're not going to puke, are you, man?" Mason asks, taking a step back.

Dylan shakes his head. "I don't think so."

"Listen," Joe says, "I know this was hard. But the good part is that somewhere a wife or a mother or a brother is going to know what happened to someone they love. That's going to help."

"I didn't think of that," Dylan says.

"And you'll have so much cred at school," Mason says. "You touched a dead body, dude!"

Joe gives him a look of such withering scorn that even Mason is cowed. "Considering the circumstances, I'm not going to bust any of you today," Joe says. "But if I ever hear of someone diving off the deck of a restaurant again, I'm bypassing the ticket and throwing you in jail."

Just then, a pickup truck roars into the parking lot.

Dylan looks relieved. "That's my dad."

"I'll talk to him." Joe walks over and speaks quietly to Mr. Brewer, who just keeps nodding at Joe and shooting glances out to the gray bay and then back at his son. He looks totally freaked. Finally, Dylan hands the blanket back to Zed and goes off with his father. The rest of the guys get into Mason's car.

Zed stands, holding the blanket against his chest. "I really have to get inside."

"Thanks for everything," I say.

"I didn't do anything." Zed frowns. "I should have stopped him from diving."

"You can't stop that pea brain from anything," Diego says. "Come on, Gracie. Let's go home."

I say good-bye to Zed, and Joe walks us to the car.

"Are they . . . going to bring it up now?" I ask.

"Yeah," Joe says. "You really don't want to be here. Trust me."

Marigold shudders. "I just want to go home."

Diego and Marigold get in the car, but I hesitate, my hand on the door handle. "It's a man, isn't it?"

"How do you know?"

Because I saw him thrashing. Because I felt his fear.

"Because you said a wife would be worrying."

"He drowned, most likely. Got snagged on some old lobster traps on the bottom."

"But it's so late in the year to go swimming. We barely even swim in the summertime, the water is so cold."

"Some do, though. They underestimate the cold. Probably happened over on the beach and the tides took him."

Joe sighs deeply, and I know what he's thinking. He's going to have to bring the news to somebody, somewhere. Somebody who loved this man.

I hear his voice in my head, *I hope he doesn't have kids.*

"He doesn't have kids," I say.

Joe looks startled. Then he sighs. "I really wish," he says, "you wouldn't do that."

When it comes to Joe's belief in my psychic ability, the jury is out. He no longer thinks I'm a liar, thanks to the fact that I ended up following my visions straight to a kidnapper. Of course the crazy kidnapper kidnapped me, too, but it all worked out in the end. But Joe doesn't quite believe in me, either. He thinks I have "a special sensitivity" or "good instincts." He doesn't like to believe in something he can't understand. Can't blame him for that.

"See you later," I say. I get in the car. When I twist around in the seat, Joe is still standing there staring as we pull away.

"Call me later," Marigold says. She has already gotten out, but she walks over to Diego's side to talk to him through the window. She leans in and kisses him. Again. I look out the window the other way.

"I'm sorry about before," she whispers.

"We'll work it out," he says.

"'Bye, Gracie," Marigold calls. She walks into her house at last. Diego doesn't pull out until she stands at the open doorway and waves again, then closes the door.

"Should I check your pulse?" I say. "Do you think you can survive until you see her again?"

Diego doesn't even get irritated at me. He grins. "You'll know what it's like someday, Gracie, and then I'll be laughing at you."

"I doubt it." I try to imagine myself hanging on Zed's every word. I can't. I like him, but really, there are limits. "So what was she apologizing for?"

"We're having a difference of opinion," Diego says as he pulls out onto the main road. "She doesn't want me to go to Costa Rica."

Diego put off college for a year. He's working now, but he's going to quit in February and go to Costa Rica with a relief youth group that helps villagers build houses. He'll stay for four months. He's been looking forward to it since he signed up.

"Why not?" I ask, even though I can guess the answer.

He shrugs. "She thinks when you have something good, you ride it out. You don't bail."

"You're not bailing. You have a life."

"She knows that. It's just hard for her. I'll be leaving right when her senior year heats up. The prom and everything."

"Oh, now I see," I say. "Villagers should go homeless so Marigold Patterson can have the date she wants for her prom."

"That's not what I meant." Diego shoots me a look. "She's not an airhead, even though you try to pretend she is. And what do you think you're doing, flirting with Zed? He's too old for you."

"He's nineteen."

"Exactly. You're fifteen."

"I'm sixteen!"

"You're a young sixteen."

"You're dating Marigold, and she's still in high school."

"Yeah, but she's eighteen."

"If I were you, I'd concentrate on my own love life," I say. "I don't criticize Marigold to you."

"No, you just sigh and roll your eyes all the time. You make your opinion pretty clear."

"Well, you obviously need an intervention. She's culted you."

"That's not even a word."

"No, but it's a fact," I say. "It's just like you're in some kind of weird Marigold-worshipping cult. You can't admit that anything is wrong with her."

"You don't like her because she's beautiful," he says. "She can't help that."

"And her brother is an idiot," I grouse.

"I can't argue with that one. But she can't help that, either. Look, I'm not asking you to like her," Diego says sharply. "I'm just asking you to shut up."

"Then you can shut up about Zed, too," I say. This is a weird conversation. In a way, it makes me feel kind of good, because it's a step forward that we're close enough to tell each other to shut up. But in another way, we're still telling each other to shut up.

When I first moved in with Diego and Shay, I was an extremely unpleasant person to be around. I was scared and angry, and mostly afraid of trusting anyone, even my relatives. I thought that my grandparents, who had been taking care of me, just unloaded me on my aunt. What I didn't know was that my aunt had fought to have me.

I'm better now. Part of that is because Diego has been incredibly cool to me, and Shay has really made me feel at home. You know somewhere is home when you start trying to get out of doing the dishes and somebody says, "No way, weasel." The minute Diego started to tease me, I knew things would be okay.

Diego pulls into the driveway. Another car is parked there, a beige Volvo that I don't recognize.

"Did Shay say we were having a guest for dinner?" I ask.

"No, but you never know with her," Diego says. "She lives to feed."

The front door opens, as if someone has been waiting for us. A man walks out. He's tall and handsome, about Shay's age, with dark hair and eyes. I wonder if Shay is two-timing Joe, but I can't imagine that, because every time he leaves, she closes the door, leans against it, and says, "I'm smitten."

"Who's that?" I ask Diego.

"No idea."

I open the door and get out. The man walks toward me. There is something about his face that I know.

I begin to feel really, really nervous.

He stops a few yards away. Behind him, Shay

appears in the doorway. She lifts a hand like a traffic cop. Is she waving at us, or trying to stop him?

"Gracie?" he says.

"Yeah?" I say.

"It's Dad," he says.

"Whose dad?" I say. I'm trying to process what he's saying, and then I know, with a sick feeling in my stomach. It's *my* dad.

The dad who left when I was three years old. The dad who never wrote and never called. The dad I never wanted to see again.

The dad I had imagined was dead.

THREE

"Let's all go into the house," Shay says.

I notice that Shay and Diego have come up on either side of me. I can feel Shay's agitation, and I know she isn't happy to see Nate.

That's my father. A man called Nate.

"Do you want to go for a walk, Gracie?" Nate asks.

"No, Nate," Shay says sharply. "Give her some room."

"I'm giving her the whole outdoors, Shay," my dad says pleasantly.

I'm so confused. I feel dizzy, as if I can feel the earth's rotation.

"This is turning out to be quite a day," Diego says.

I look at Shay. "Can we just go inside?"

"Of course, sweetie." Shay puts her arm around me and keeps it there as we walk toward the house.

We sit in the living room. The house is small, but it has so many windows that it never feels dark or claustrophobic. To one side of the fireplace is a sofa with deep cushions, and facing it are two big, comfortable armchairs. In the middle is a table that we sometimes eat around on cold nights.

Nate picks the sofa and looks encouragingly at me, and I know he wants me to sit next to him. I sit in one of the armchairs. Shay sits in the other chair, and Diego leans against the wall.

"I apologize for not calling," Nate says to me. "I was going to. And then I was just going to drive by first, just to see . . . and Shay was outside, and she saw me."

"Why did you come?" I ask.

"I heard about your mother."

I shake my head. "It's been two years."

"I know. There was no way for me to know, Gracie. I would have come right away if I'd known."

"Let me get this straight," I say. "You don't come for my birthdays, you don't come when I'm sick, you don't come for thirteen years, but you would have shown up for a funeral?"

Nate shakes his head. "Okay, I deserved that."

"You're darn right you did," Shay murmurs.

"Oh, please," I say. "Listen, you didn't have to show up. You could have called. Or sent me an e-mail."

"There's so much to tell you," Nate says.

"Yeah, me, too," I say. "I was three years old when you left. A few things have happened."

I'm trying not to have it all come back to me, but it's flooding in, and I'm holding myself together because I just might fall apart. I am thinking of the years. The years before I was able to just wipe the notion of "father" out of my life. Watching other kids with their dads. Imagining him knocking on the door. Closing my eyes and picturing it. And mostly, seeing a three-year-old girl with her dad, seeing how the father holds her hand, or picks her up, or leans down to talk to her . . . and thinking, *How could he do it? How could he leave me?*

Mom had always said that Dad was a "complicated man." When I was little, she'd just say he loved me very much . . . and leave it at that. But later, she would tell me sometimes that she'd loved him despite the "better angels of my nature." When she quoted Abraham Lincoln, you knew it was serious stuff.

Nate stands up. "I know this must be a shock to you. Maybe it's better that the first visit be short, so you can process this."

Shay stands up quickly. "That's a good idea. What do you think, Gracie?"

I'm picking up so much turmoil from Shay. She hates having Nate in this house. I can feel it. Is she afraid of him? Afraid he'll snatch me away? Afraid I'll go with him?

"That might be best," I say.

"Will you walk me to the car?" Nate asks me.

I look at him, really look at him, for the first time. He's always been not quite a person to me.

Now I see . . . myself. I always thought I looked like my mom. She always told me I did, too. But now I know she was lying. Lying to protect me. Because I wouldn't have wanted to know how much I looked like him.

And that pulls me out the door with him, somehow.

The front door thuds behind us. It sends a shudder through me, as though it's cut me off from Shay and Diego forever. Since we've been sitting inside, dusk has fallen, and the light is deep blue and smudgy with shadows.

"My own dad was manic-depressive," Nate says. "Your grandfather. He died when I was in college. He killed himself. They didn't diagnose him correctly, I guess. He lived in terror for a lot of the time, and he tried not to take it out on us, but he did."

Well. Nate sure didn't believe in small talk.

"I never felt I was loved, growing up," Nate continues. "I mean, I don't want to boo-hoo all over you. That could get messy." He flashes an uneasy smile. "I'm just trying to explain a little bit of why it took me so long to get myself together. Only one person in my life really loved me as a child, and that was my aunt Jane. I was afraid I would grow up to be my father. After you were born, it all crashed down on me, all that fear. I was terrified I'd turn you into something you wouldn't want to be, Gracie."

I realize that I'm holding my breath so I won't miss a word.

"I was afraid I'd turn you into me," he says.

I don't look at him. I look at my shoes. I look at every individual blade of grass, because if this is an apology, it just isn't doing it for me.

"Some mornings I couldn't get out of bed," he says. "I thought — *It's happening to me. I'm going to ruin Carrie's life, and Gracie's life. They'll be better off without me.* I'll tell you. If you get to the place where you think the people you love most in the world are better off without you . . . well, it's a very bad place."

He starts walking again, and I walk beside him, listening now.

"I went to New Mexico because I didn't know anyone there and nobody knew me," he says. "I found a therapist. After some treatment — well, eventually, I got better. I found out I'm not manic-depressive. Just screwed up. And I worked on my problems, and when I got clear, I realized . . ." He swallows, and his voice cracks. "I'd blown it. It was too late. I couldn't just walk back into my own front door. It wasn't my home any longer. I lost any right to think that. And I was a coward, and so I kept . . . putting it off. *I'll call on her birthday,* I'd say. Or Christmas. Or summertime. And months went by, and years . . . and I remembered what a therapist had told me — *If you can't be there every day for her, don't do it. She'll be better off.*"

He stops, his hand on the car door. "I think you were better off without me. That's the honest truth."

"So what's different now?" I ask.

"I met someone. I got married. And she wants to have kids. And my track record . . . well, I just thought, I already have a kid. I don't want to be one of those dads who has a second family and forgets he ever had a first. And my wife . . . she's a good person. She's the one who pointed out to me that I couldn't be a father to a new child if I didn't try again with the child I had."

"So she told you to come here. You wouldn't have come otherwise." For some reason, that makes me furious.

He lets out a breath. "I'm not going to lie to you, Gracie. That's true. But what you have to know is, Rachel makes me do a lot of things I didn't think I was capable of doing. She makes me a better person. I want to live up to what she thinks I am." He pauses and then he says, "I'd like you to meet her sometime."

I hear in his voice a hopefulness that makes me angry . . . and sad, too. Does he really think that he can come here and make everything else go away?

"I don't think so," I say.

"Well." He clears his throat. "I'm going to hang around for a few more days. I'll call tomorrow and, if you want, I'd like to take you to lunch. Or anything."

"I'll see," I say. It's as much as I can give him, and it feels like too much.

FOUR

I let the door shut behind me when I walk back into the house. The living room is dark now. Shay and Diego are in the kitchen. I smell something funny, something I've never smelled in Shay's house. It's unpleasant. I wrinkle my nose.

Underneath my feet the hardwood floor feels spongy. I smell mildew and stale air and I want to cough, but I can't seem to catch a breath of pure air. . . .

And suddenly, I realize I'm having a vision, and I'm trapped in the vision, and I can't get out, and I can't breathe, and there's a roaring in my ears. . . .

Shay turns on the light, and the living room springs forward, all comfortable and warm. I feel my hammering heart.

"I thought I'd light a fire," she says.

"That would be good," I say. I tell my heart to slow down.

What had I seen? Was it Shay's house or another house?

Did it have to do with the drowned man? Or my father?

By the time Shay has placed the kindling and

waddcd up newspapers and built her foolproof-fire system, my heart rate has returned to the normal range. I curl up on the couch and reach for the wool throw that's folded on the back. I pull it over my legs and sit back against the sofa arm so I can look at the flames.

Shay sits down opposite me. Her dark, curly hair is pulled back in a ponytail and she's in her floppy fleece pants, so I guess she's not seeing Joe tonight. Since she's been dating Joe, Shay's wardrobe has improved to an amazing degree. She's a little overweight, round and pretty, and she's started wearing filmy blouses and velvet pants instcad of her denim shirts and jeans. She's even exchanged Chap Stick for lip gloss.

"You look pretty shaken," she says. "I know I was."

"I just don't get what he wants."

"He wants to know you, sweetie." Shay pats my leg. "Diego told me about Dylan Brewer. You poor baby, what a day. How do you feel?"

Here is the part where I'm supposed to share my feelings. Sometimes having a family is hard. What I want to do is look at the fire and zone out. I don't want to talk about my feelings. I just want to ignore them until they go away.

After my mother was killed in the car crash, I had to go to something called "grief counseling." I hated it at the time, but I came to have a great deal of respect for Dr. Alison Politsky. I learned that telling someone how you feel doesn't mean you'll fall apart and won't be able to put yourself back together again. I learned that it's possible to put yourself back together again, one piece at a time.

Dr. Politsky showed me the road map. Shay put me on the road.

So even though at this particular moment I don't want to talk about my father, I do.

"I feel angry and sad and confused and sick to my stomach," I say. "I feel like telling him to go away forever. But I know I should at least hear him out."

Shay squeezes my knee. "You don't have to do anything you don't want to do. I have his address. You can always contact him when you're ready. You don't have to be on his timetable."

That was true. I hadn't thought about it that way. "He wants to have lunch tomorrow."

"Do you want to?"

"I don't know."

"So sleep on it. I have an idea. Joe had to cancel, so it's just us for dinner tonight. I'm making black bean chili and cornbread for dinner. Then let's watch some really goofy DVD. Diego has a date with Marigold."

I groan, and Shay smacks me on the knee playfully. "Shhh," she warns.

"I just can't get used to her," I whisper.

"I know."

"I just don't understand him."

Shay shrugs. "What you need to know, honey, is that sometimes you can fall for someone you don't even like very much. I think that might have happened to Diego."

"But he defends her all the time."

"A little too much, I think. I think he's trying to convince himself, too."

There's a knock at the door. Shay and I both look at the door as if there's a werewolf behind it. We're both afraid that Nate has come back.

"Don't let him in," I say.

"We don't know it's him," she murmurs. She gets up and answers the door.

I hear Joe's voice saying hello.

"I thought you canceled," Shay says. "Because if you didn't, I'm busted. I'm wearing my very oldest sweatpants. Don't look."

"Gross," Joe says. "But I'm afraid I'm here in an official capacity. Is Diego around?"

"Is it about that poor drowned guy?"

"Shay," Joe says, "did you hear me say *official*?"

"Oh. Yeah."

"Then can you not kiss me when you say that?"

I smile, and a moment later Joe walks in. Shay hollers for Diego, and I say hello.

"How are you doing?" Joe comes closer to give me the once-over.

"I'm okay. It's not like I saw anything."

Diego walks in the room. "Hi, Joe."

"It's official business," Shay says.

"Hi, Detective Pasta," Diego says.

Before we knew Joe Fusilli, before he practically became a member of the family, we used to call him Detective Pasta. It must be hard to be named after a curly noodle, even though Joe claims an ancestor of his invented it.

"There was a break-in and some malicious mischief on a house down in the new development," Joe says.

Frowning, Shay moves a little closer to Diego.

"I don't think you did it, Diego," Joe says. "But did you hear any kids boasting about it? It seems like some kind of prank, and I know that crowd you hang with now doesn't like the weekend people."

"Look, Mason is a bit of a jerk, but he wouldn't do something like that," Diego says.

"Tempers are running high because of Hassam's Farm," Joe says.

Diego nods. "I know."

"Mason's best friend is Andy Hassam. Mason has worked at the farm stand."

"I've worked there, too," Diego says. "Practically every kid in this area has had a summer job there."

"Did anyone steal anything in the break-in?" Shay asks. I can tell she's trying to turn the conversation, because Diego is starting to look angry.

"No. The house is empty. It was just sold — or, at least, someone put a bid on it. A Seattle businessman," Joe says. "I'm just looking at the resentment factor. His name is Hank Hobbs."

I see Shay start at the name. Joe, who never misses anything, sees it, too.

"You know him?"

"Sure," Shay says. "He's a major contributor to the wetlands reclamation project. We almost had to shut it down last month until he pledged a million dollars."

Shay is a scientist with a special interest in wetlands. She works for an environmental company here on Beewick. Their major project for the past four years has been the restoration of this wetland area on Beewick, down near the ferry on the southern part of the island. Twenty years ago, a corporation, Monvor Industries, polluted and flooded the land. The final part of the restoration is scheduled for next week, when the last of the land will be drained.

"Maybe Hobbs was targeted," Shay says. "He was once vice president of Monvor. He's contributed to the reclamation project out of guilt, I imagine. But maybe somebody found out about his connection to the original pollution. It hasn't been publicized; he wanted to keep things quiet. Have you talked to him?"

"I've got a call in to him," Joe says.

The timer goes off in the kitchen. "That's my cornbread," Shay says. "Do you want to stay for dinner?"

Joe shakes his head wearily. "I'm still waiting for lab results. We still haven't IDed the body."

"I'll take out the cornbread," Diego says, and heads for the kitchen.

"I'll help," I say. I trail after Diego while Shay walks Joe to the door.

Diego puts on oven mittens and still manages to look fairly manly. He wrestles the cast-iron pan full of cornbread out of the oven and kicks the door shut with his foot. I start taking down plates to set the table.

"So?" I say.

"So, what?"

"So, did you tell Joe the truth, or do you know who vandalized the house?"

Diego is busy sliding the hot pan onto a trivet. He throws the oven mitts down.

"Of course I don't know," he says.

"Are you sure it wasn't Mason and his dinosaur pals? They definitely have it in for the weekenders."

"They're not idiots," Diego says. "They wouldn't do that."

Wouldn't they? Diego is so deluded that he thinks Marigold has an interesting mind. He's completely head over heels.

How far would he go to protect her brother?

FIVE

Sometimes just a question will rock a household, even if the answer is what you want to hear. I can tell that Shay is worried about the crowd Diego is hanging with. Diego is a pretty independent guy, so it's unusual that he's spending all this time with Marigold's brother.

The fact that my father has suddenly shown up hasn't made things any easier. When he calls on Sunday, I tell him I'm busy. I'm just not ready to deal with it. Not yet. Maybe not ever.

But even though I tell him I'm not ready, I still think about him all day, so what's the point? I can feel his presence on the island. I wonder what else he has to tell me. I wonder if I can ever ask the questions that burn me up inside. I know he's staying at the inn in Greystone Harbor, and so I stick close to home all afternoon. I don't want to run into him in town.

Shay has to work on Sunday afternoon, and Diego is off with Marigold, so I take out the photo album my mom made for me. I don't have that many photos of my dad in it, but I've memorized every one.

There is one I used to look at all the time, taken before they were married. He's at the beach, and he's wearing a dark T-shirt and loose khaki pants. They're rolled up at the ankles. He's sitting in the sand, his hands around his knees. The wind is blowing his hair, and he's laughing. Really laughing. This is the photograph that used to break me, because he looks so happy. So handsome. So much like a dad someone would want.

What is real? How much of what I see is influenced by how I feel? Do I want my father to be bad, or good?

I am a person who already has problems with reality. I see things that aren't there. But my psychic ability isn't going to help me figure out my own life — it doesn't work that way. It just confuses things more. I don't know if the feelings I'm picking up from him are true or not. I don't know if the yearning I felt in him the other night is real.

I flip through the pages of the album. When I was born, my mom and dad lived in a tiny house in Maryland, on the Eastern Shore. There's one photograph that my mom said my dad took of me. I'm probably about two, I guess. I'm sitting on the lawn, wearing my mom's hat, which makes me look like a baby version of the Cat in the Hat. My father picked the wrong place to stand, because the sun is casting his shadow on the lawn next to me. Some of his shadow lies over me.

It always has. It's all I ever had of him — a shadow. Now I have the real thing, the real man, the one I've hated. The one I've loved. The one who broke my life into two pieces.

I close the book. I'd rather have the pictures, have the shadow. The man is too real.

It's late when Shay struggles in the door, carrying grocery bags. I run forward to help her. We go toward the back of the house and put the grocery bags on the counter. Instead of unpacking them, Shay plops down in a kitchen chair, still in her coat.

"Founders Realty was vandalized last night," she says.

"What did the vandals do?"

"Threw some files on the floor, put trash on the desks, unplugged the little refrigerator, stuff like that," Shay says. "Joe says it's like they didn't want to do too much damage to push it into a serious crime, which sounds like —"

"Teenagers," I say. "Do you think it could be Mason?"

Shay shrugs out of her coat. "Diego has always been sort of idiot-proof," she says. "I mean, even as a kid, he knew what kids to avoid. He's got a good head on his shoulders. But he's in love. Sometimes you're looking so hard at who you love that . . . you miss things. Big things. Because you're trying to fit your love into the kind of thing you want it to be."

"Is he really in love with Marigold?" I ask.

Shay smiles gently. "Yeah. Look, Gracie, I'm as surprised as you are that it's this girl. But love is love. He's got to go through it. And we have to stay out of it."

She says this last part with meaning, and I nod slowly. "I guess I haven't been so nice about Marigold sometimes."

"So I hear. Let's just try to keep our mouths shut and support him, okay?"

"Okay."

"Joe will find out who's doing this. That's his job. Not ours. Your job is to do your homework, and my job is to get through this next few weeks with my job, and then we'll all be happy again. Right?"

"Absolutely." We smile at each other. We've been talking in the dark. It reminds me of the early mornings we once spent together, when I first moved here and wasn't talking to anyone. When I'd wake up in a panic, I'd sit in the kitchen, and somehow Shay would know I was awake, and come and join me. She wouldn't say a word, just pad around the kitchen warming up milk and cups until my crying stopped. She wouldn't even touch me. She knew if she'd touched me, I'd run back in my room. So she'd make hot chocolate, and we'd sit in silence, sipping the hot drink, and watching the light turn from navy to deep blue. And then, still without saying a word, I'd wash the cups and the milk pan, and we'd both go back to bed.

I have this, I think. *I don't need him. I have this.*

"Well, I'm going to take a shower, and then start dinner," Shay says. "Maybe trays in front of the fire tonight. I'm beat." She heads for her room, stretching as she goes.

I head to my room, which used to be a mudroom that Shay and Diego had fixed up for me. I reach out for the light switch, but for a moment, I get disoriented. I'm not seeing the room as it is, with glass panes. I see a broken screen, blowing. I see a door where a window is now.

And I smell that smell again, mildew and rot and staleness, as if the house had been shut up for years and years. I can't find the light switch, and my heart is pounding, and suddenly I feel terror well up in me, because the floor is sticky underneath my feet.

I see it in flashes. Footprints on floorboards, the outline smudged and rusty-looking.

Blood. Someone walked in the blood.

Clean it up clean it up clean it up . . .

A bloody towel.

The smell of it in the house.

"No!" I shout, and I step back, my hand desperately scrabbling for the light switch. Light floods the room, and it's just my room again, with the headboard painted yellow and the blue floor and the patterned curtains. I can hear Shay in the shower, singing a Joni Mitchell song.

I sink down on the bed and grab my pillow and squeeze it.

I don't want to see what I see.

I want it to go away.

I know that whatever it was that I saw — past or future — was murder.

SIX

It started when I was ten, when I almost drowned at the beach in Maryland. A lifeguard rescued me, and when I came to, I could hear what she was thinking.

I didn't tell anyone but my mom. She almost got me tested, but somehow we always found excuses not to. I think we just hoped it would go away. I know I did.

I could never read my mom, and I never got flashes about her, but the day she died was the worst day of my life, even before my grandparents showed up at the door to give me the news. I sat on the couch all day, knowing something was wrong. I stared at the phone and couldn't move.

I was smelling oranges that day, and I didn't know why. I felt like I couldn't breathe, and I didn't know why.

Then I heard she was hit by a truck carrying oranges. That she was choking on her own blood. And I knew why.

Even today, the smell of orange juice makes me sick.

Whatever this ability I have is, it's not

something I can shut off like a faucet. It sneaks up on me. It comes when I least expect it, when I'm eating ice cream or sitting in the car or listening to the principal read the school announcements. And then I know that the girl behind the ice cream counter is worried because her boss is hitting on her, or the man on the bike stopping to wipe his forehead at the stoplight is short of breath because there's something wrong with his heart, and the principal wants a divorce but is afraid of what would happen to her kids if she went through with it.

I don't want to know these things.

And I don't want to walk into my room and see a river of blood on the floor.

I don't want to walk through the house and feel spooked. But that's what happens. I see something out of the corner of my eye. Something I'll catch if I turn quickly enough. A shadow. An outflung hand. A spreading stain on the floor, a pool of blood.

I'm afraid of being alone in the house.

School is school. Some days it's not too bad, and other days it makes you want to run shrieking into the wilderness.

Beewick High squashes kids from three towns into one school, and it's still small. Everyone has known each other since preschool, so I felt a little left out at the beginning. I got befriended by Emily Carbonel, but she was kidnapped last year. I think what we went through together drove us apart instead of bringing us closer. I think I just remind her of what she went through. This year she's turned into a skittish, nervous geek who never takes off her earphones from her MP-3 player, which kind of reminds me of me last year, actually. Sometimes kids talk to me, and I have a few class-room friendships, but nobody is inviting me home for soda and pretzels.

My rep has not improved since everyone found out I get psychic flashes. You can break down reactions into three areas:

1. You're so weird. Are you reading my mind right now?
2. Can you see the questions on tomorrow's test in your mind?
3. Can you tell me if Jason really, really likes me?

You see, the thing is, when you're in high school, you have secrets. You have crushes, you have thoughts, you want things you shouldn't want. And if you're afraid someone can see inside you, you don't slide your tray next to hers at lunch.

I wish I could tell them that I can't see inside them. My flashes are unpredictable. The closer I am to someone, the murkier they are. For example, I can't tell what my aunt Shay is thinking just about one hundred percent of the time if she doesn't want me to. Diego is as much of a mystery to me as any boy.

And then there's dear old Dad. I won't even bother trying to figure him out.

After school, I stuff my books into my backpack, taking my time while I do it. I'm stalling for two reasons. One, I'm afraid to go home. Two, I always do. Everyone congregates outside on the steps after school. Plans are made, promises to call, running jokes. I don't want to have to walk through that, so I usually wait until kids have headed off to their cars or into town.

It's a gloomy, wet day. I decide to go to the town library and do my homework. If I stretch it out long enough, I can walk home and Shay will be just getting home from work. Diego works late on Mondays.

When I come out of school, Nate is sitting on the stone column at the bottom of the railing, just like kids do. He's got a paper cone of French fries from the Bluebay Drive-In, which has the best fries in the known universe.

He holds out the cone to me. "I thought you might need a ride home."

I ignore the French fries, even though the smell of them makes my stomach growl. "I'm not going home. I'm going to the library."

He jumps down. "The library, then."

"It's two blocks away."

"I think I can manage it." He swings into step beside me. "So. I have a proposal. We each get three questions we can ask each other. And we have to tell the truth."

"I don't want to —"

"Here's my first one. Do you want these or not?" He holds up the cone.

"No."

"Liar." He holds them out, but I refuse to take one. It will feel like some kind of surrender.

He shrugs. It is with some regret that I watch the full cone of fries sail into the garbage can.

"That was my best bribe," he says. He puts his hands in his pockets. "Okay, go ahead. Your turn."

"Are you still a lawyer?"

"No. I left the law when I left Maryland. I always hated it."

"What do you do now?"

"My last job was in commercial real estate. Before that . . . a bunch of things. I sold houses in Santa Fe. Wrote a newspaper column once. Oh, and I ran a surf shop in San Diego. That was fun."

Great. While he was having fun on the beach, I was growing up fatherless.

"Where do you live now?"

"Wallanan. It's right outside of Tacoma."

I stop. "Tacoma?" For almost a whole year, he's been less than two hours away.

He stops, too, and looks me full in the face. "I didn't know you were here, on Beewick, until last week."

We both breathe in and out, passing through the moment.

"Look," he continues. "I came here to tell you that if you want me to leave, I'll leave. But I also came here to tell you that even if I leave, I'll keep trying. Brace yourself for birthday cards, kiddo."

We continue down the hill into town. And I have such a weird moment of feeling normal. *Here is my dad, and we're walking into town.* As if all my heartbreak had never been.

And then the normal moment is gone, and I'm walking with the man who abandoned me and my mother. My whole body stiffens up again.

"The thing is," he says, "I have a lot to catch up on. So I thought I'd start with these." He hands me a stack of envelopes.

"What are these?" I ask, but I know what they are. Thirteen birthday cards. One for every year he missed.

He leaves me at the library steps without a word. I take out my books, but I spend most of my time there looking through the cards. He's chosen them carefully, I see. Each one is age-appropriate.

One after the other. Blues Clues. Dora the Explorer. Birthday cakes. Balloons. Sailboats. And then sentimental ones, near the end. Signed at the bottom of each is a message: *Love, Dad.*

There's something sort of goofy about the gesture. It should really piss me off, but it doesn't. And for some reason, it doesn't make me sad. Maybe it's because he chose such stupid cards. I can't help smiling.

The light is dimming outside, and I know it's time to leave. The other kids here have left long ago, and the moms with toddlers. Everyone wants to go home to dinner. And I'm still stalling.

Joy the librarian stands behind my chair, holding a stack of books. She leans in close to my ear.

"Murder will out."

Her breath on the back of my neck makes me start and pull away.

"What?" I ask, twisting around.

She nods significantly, except I don't know what the significance is. The fluorescent lights overhead shine in the frames of her glasses, and I can't see her eyes.

"Murderers get caught. He's on Beewick somewhere, with his normal face. But he'll be caught."

I realize now she's trying to reassure me. Because I was around when the body was found. But instead, she just creeps me out.

"Thanks," I say.

I walk home slowly in the dusk. When I open the door, I smell the fire and feel the warmth. I know the smell of this house now in my bones — of the beeswax Shay rubs on the wood floors, the floors she refinished herself when she bought the house, after tearing up the thick shag carpeting. Every house has a smell, and this house is starting to smell like home. I want to grab on to this feeling and ride it. I want to make it the one true thing I have. But I can't.

I wake up on Tuesday morning early. I hear noise in the kitchen, and when I walk out, Shay is already up. Papers are stacked on the kitchen table, and she's going through them, frowning.

"Work?" I ask as I pour myself some cereal.

"What? Oh. Problems, as usual," Shay groans. She looks at the clock and jumps up in a panic. "I have a meeting!"

"At seven in the morning?"

"Seven-thirty, and I haven't showered. . . . Oh, I'll be so glad when this project is over," Shay moans. She runs out, the belt of her bathrobe trailing behind her.

I chomp on my cereal. The papers are still spread out on the table, so I reach over to put them back in the file for Shay. She'll probably need them for the meeting, and in this state, she'll probably just run out the door without them if I don't remind her.

DEED OF SALE

I read the words upside down.

17 Fieldstone Lane.

This house. Why was Shay looking at the papers for this house? She bought it twenty years ago. I turn the deed around. I can't believe how cheap the house was, but Shay has told me what a wreck it was when she found it.

My eyes travel down to the bottom, where the owner's signature is.

SHAY MILLICENT KENZIE

NATHANIEL G. MILLAR

Nate? My father?

My father owns the house with Shay?

I can't believe what I'm reading. I look at the date. I know I was born about three years after my parents got married. That means that Shay knew my father before my mother did. Knew him well enough to buy a house with him.

I drop the spoon into the bowl. Milk splashes over the rim.

Shay has been hiding this from me.

Shay, who I thought was the most honest person I know.

Shay, who always told me that hiding your feelings can backfire.

Shay is as big a liar as dear old Dad.

SEVEN

When Shay comes out in her work clothes with her hair wet, I'm still sitting at the table. She starts hunting for her keys. "I hope they have bagels at this meeting. And coffee. Definitely coffee —"

She sees my face and stops. "What is it?" Her gaze travels to the papers on the table.

"You lied to me," I say.

"Not really," she says carefully.

I slam my hand down. "You *lied* to me!"

"Oh, honey, no, no. It just never . . . when I would bring up your dad, you would always just shut down. So I thought . . . one step at a time."

"So when were you going to tell me he owns half of this house? Is that why you took me in? Because you thought he'd come back and want the house, and if I was living here, he couldn't turn you out on the street?" I don't know where that idea came from, but suddenly it blazed across my brain. I feel tears sting my eyes, and I will them to go away.

Shay looks shocked. "No! No, of course not!" She puts her briefcase on the chair. "We need to talk about this."

"You have a meeting. It can wait." I turn away to go back into my room.

"No, it can't."

She picks up the phone and calls someone. I hear her murmur something about a family emergency.

"You're a pretty cool liar, Shay," I say after she hangs up. "I didn't think you could lie to save your life."

"That wasn't a lie. This *is* a family emergency. Will you sit down, Gracie?"

I don't want to sit. I want to run. I want to run and run and run until the blood pounding in my ears drives out every thought in my head.

But I also want answers, so I sit.

"Were you a couple?" I ask her. "You and Nate?"

"No, we were never a couple. We were friends. Let me start at the beginning," Shay says. "I met Nate a long time ago in Seattle, where I was living at the time. I had dropped out of grad school and was working as a waitress, and I joined this environmental group. We heard about what Monvor was doing up here, destroying the wetlands, and a bunch of us decided to come up here one summer and camp out for a month and do protests." Shay shrugs. "We were young. It seemed like a good idea at the time."

She pushes back her hair. "Well, we didn't

really accomplish anything. We did a few protests that made the papers. But mostly we sat around talking about the best way to shut down Monvor, then went hiking and swimming. Some of us were more committed than others. I'd say that Nate was our unofficial leader. He was so charismatic. We all looked up to him. He had these great ideas — but in the end, we all just drifted apart."

"What about the house?"

"I fell in love with Beewick Island that summer," Shay says. "I saw myself here. And real estate was really cheap. I had saved some money, and I thought if some of us chipped in and bought a house, we could all share it on weekends. Dumb idea, by the way. Two others in the group were interested. One dropped out, and that left me and Nate. We found this house, and we bought it. Carrie came out to help me with the sale — she had just graduated from law school. That's when she met Nate. I saw it happen the moment they met — they fell in love instantly. They were married six months later. So half of the house really belonged to your mother, too. She had a good career, and she didn't need the money, so even though I offered to buy her out a couple of times, she refused. She knew it was hard for me to come up with the money. And I wouldn't let her just give me half the house, either. It was just something between us, and we never thought . . . we never thought it would matter one way or another."

I absorb this. It makes sense. I knew my mother had met Nate out here. I'd never wanted the details.

This is what happens when you don't want details. They pile up and pile up, and then you get them all at once, and they knock you right over.

But I get the feeling that there are holes in this story. Things Shay isn't telling me. Usually, I can't read Shay. But somehow I'm picking up flashes.

"Apples," I say. "What is it about apples?"

"Apples?"

"And a . . . a gate?"

Shay goes pale.

The door has opened, but we haven't heard it. Joe is standing in the kitchen doorway.

"Yes, Shay," he says. "Tell us about William Applegate."

EIGHT

Shay looks up at Joe. Then she glances at me. I can tell this is something she doesn't want to talk about in front of me. Or maybe, I suddenly realize, she doesn't want to talk about it with Joe.

"Billy," she says, her voice faint. "We called him Billy. He was one of us. When we decided to disband the group, he disappeared. I don't know what happened to him. Neither did his family. They never discovered what happened."

"Imagine my surprise," Joe says, "when I ran Hank Hobbs through our computers and discovered that you tried to bring charges against him for the murder of William Applegate."

"It was a long time ago," Shay says.

"And six weeks ago, Hank Hobbs tried to get you fired from the wetlands project. Said he wouldn't give a contribution unless they fired you. There is a million dollars at stake."

Shay smiles faintly. "I guess he held a grudge."

"You never told me about it."

"It was a work problem."

I am watching both of them carefully. They are

speaking in low voices, but I can feel Joe's anger and Shay's fear.

"Why don't you tell me about it now," Joe says, and I realize with a chill that he has his professional voice on. Shay is no dummy; she feels it, too.

"Billy was always so intense," she says. "We all took our environmental work seriously, but for Billy, it was like life and death. He used to get so angry when anybody would goof off, when we'd go swimming or have a softball game. He used to browbeat us about our lack of commitment. So he wasn't exactly popular with the group."

Joe sits down at the table. "Go on."

"Then we had this breakthrough. Billy somehow got his hands on a secret file that showed that Monvor had falsified data regarding outflow pollutants. There was going to be an inquiry, and they decided to stonewall it by producing a false set of data. Billy had the file in his duffel. But then our campsite was burgled, and the evidence was stolen along with some personal items. We all had a huge argument. Billy basically accused someone — he didn't know who — in the group of betraying us and stealing the file. Everyone was furious, and that was the beginning of the end. The group just fell apart. We had no evidence to expose Monvor, and we weren't even friends anymore. Billy just . . . he went ballistic. This was the end of everything he'd worked for. That night, he took me aside. He told me he was going to Monvor's headquarters to confront Hank Hobbs. He believed that Hobbs had bribed one of us to destroy the file. He left. I never saw him again."

"And when the police investigated, you pointed them to Hobbs."

"Of course," Shay says. "That's where he was headed. But I don't know . . . it was soon after that I put everything together. I think Billy might have committed suicide. Or else he just took off. He was truly troubled, and his relations with his family . . . they weren't the greatest. I really don't think he was murdered. I don't think I believed it at the time. I was caught up in it all, and I don't think I was thinking straight. Now, I'm embarrassed at accusing Hank Hobbs. I think that's one reason I never told you about this, Joe."

The light has been growing for some time now, and sunshine is beginning to streak through the windows into the kitchen.

"Why did you come here, Joe?" Shay asks. "Why are you interested in Billy Applegate now?"

"Because the drowned body has been identified," Joe says. "It's Hank Hobbs."

NINE

Shay goes white. "Was he murdered?"

"We don't know," Joe says. "We know he couldn't swim. The Coast Guard found the boat out in the Sound."

"He has a boat, and he can't swim?" I ask.

"It happens," Joe says, in that way he has of showing that there isn't anything on earth he hasn't seen or heard about. "It looks like he slipped and fell, possibly sustaining a head injury. Or that could have happened after he'd been knocking around the rocks in the harbor."

Shay and I both wince.

"Anyway," Joe says briskly, "we'll know more after the autopsy."

"Was the dinghy missing?"

Joe turns to me. "No." He looks surprised that I would think of that, but it was the first question that popped into my head.

"But if he was murdered, how did the killer get away?"

"There could have been two boats," Joe says. "Or the killer could have swum to shore. It's possible. The tides are tricky, but you can do it."

Shay has gone very still. "Am I a suspect, Joe?" she asks.

"Nobody's a suspect," he says. "I don't know if he was murdered. I'm just looking for background."

"Oh. Because you're acting like I'm a suspect."

"I'm just gathering information."

"You could be nicer about it."

Joe looks annoyed. "I'm on a case, Shay. I don't have time to hold your hand."

She's furious. He catches her anger, and chooses to ignore it. I'm watching them like a tennis match.

He turns to me. "Speaking of the case, I hear your father is in town. Why did he come?"

"He heard that my mother died," I say.

"That was two years ago."

"He was out of touch."

He turns to Shay. "Nathaniel Millard was one of the group that summer."

"He was a friend before he became my brother-in-law," Shay says in a small, tight voice that isn't like hers. "I haven't seen him since Gracie was a baby."

"Do you know where he's staying?"

"The inn in Greystone Harbor," I say. "Why?"

Joe stands. "Just gathering information," he says.

I know why Joe is going to talk to Nate. Is it just a coincidence that he's shown up, and Joe has a murdered guy on his hands?

Is this a reunion or a crime scene?

Shay drives me to school. She's gripping the steering wheel and grinding her teeth. Once, she pops out with, "'I don't have time to hold your *hand*,' he says!" Detective that I am, I get that she's thinking about Joe.

She stops in the parking lot and turns to me.

"Look," she says, "I know you feel I should have told you all this. You have to believe I was going to. I wanted to find your father first. I hired a private detective to find him."

"Why?" I couldn't believe that it was *Shay* who'd started all this.

"Because he was always out there!" Shay bursts out. "I don't know what he'd want. And the fact that this man owns half my house and could take you away from me — I couldn't sleep at night, thinking of that. I had to do something. I offered to buy him out, and he said yes. But he had to see you first."

"Buy him out?"

"Of the house," she says. "I don't want his name on the deed."

I'm just sitting there, clutching the door handle, trying to make sense of all this.

"I can't believe you didn't tell me!"

"I didn't know if I'd find him."

"Well, you found him." I can't even look at her. I'm too confused and angry. "Happy now?"

"You have every reason in the world to hate him," Shay says. "Of course. But he's just a man, Gracie. A screw-up, sure. But someone who wants to know you. Do you know, the private detective told me that when he told Nate that Carrie was dead, he broke down. He really didn't know, Gracie. Nate called me soon after. I told him not to come up, that I wanted to talk to you first, but he couldn't wait. I was shocked when he drove by. I thought I'd have time to prepare you."

"Did he know Hank Hobbs?" I ask.

"What?" Shay is startled.

"You were all there that summer. Did he know him?"

"You think he could have killed Hank Hobbs?"

"I'm just asking."

"I don't think he ever met him," Shay says. "I know I didn't. We were protesting against a company; we didn't target any individuals. Nate isn't a murderer, Gracie. I know he isn't."

"You haven't seen him in twenty years."

"I don't care. I knew him pretty well back then. He was irresponsible, obviously. Maybe not the most truthful person I ever met. But he wouldn't commit cold-blooded murder. He couldn't."

How can she be so sure? I'm not.

"I wish I hadn't started this." She blows out a breath and rests her forehead on the steering wheel for a moment. "I know I just made a mess of everything. But I was thinking of you the whole time."

"Maybe . . . maybe you should have thought a little harder," I say.

I see Shay's hands tighten on the steering wheel. "Good point," she says.

TEN

After school, I head into town. I don't want to go home yet. It has nothing to do with the fact that I happen to know that Zed works the lunch shift on Tuesdays and then has the rest of the day off. It has nothing to do with the fact that I know his shift is over right about now.

I walk slowly past the Harborside, and I hear him call my name.

He's sitting outside, one leg over his bike. He leans the bike against the railing and comes over. I wish, I wish, I wouldn't immediately go blank when I see him. I wish I could manage a witty hello. Something more interesting than "hi."

"Hi," I say.

"I'm glad I ran into you," Zed says. "That was one weird afternoon. I was wondering if you were okay."

"I'm okay," I say. "Did you hear that they identified the . . . the guy?"

"Hank Hobbs, yeah," Zed says. "It's funny, because he just had lunch at the restaurant last week. I waited on him. Creepy. Not him, but knowing that he died, like, maybe later that day."

"Who was he having lunch with?"

"Jeff Ferris. They were talking about some house he's buying in that new development over by Hassam's Farm."

"Hobbs was buying a house there?"

Zed nods. "He was buying Jeff's house. He has one on Larch Lane — prime spot, right on the water. He bought right at the beginning, before they were even built, and now he'll make a killing. Smart."

"I guess. Did Hobbs seem upset or anything?"

"No. I already talked to the police. So did Jeff. Neither of us picked up anything from Mr. Hobbs. It was a beautiful day, though. You know how the weather was so nice last week. I guess he decided to take a boat ride after lunch."

This is the most Zed has ever said to me, and I want to savor the moment, but I have an idea. The new development isn't too far; I can make it on my bike in twenty minutes. I could go out to the house on Larch Lane and poke around.

Something is pulling at me. An image of a body falling through water, sinking, spiraling down from sunlit green water into the black depths of the bay. I know now that the body I saw is Hank Hobbs.

I try to get a picture of my dad on that boat, but I can't. It's a blank.

Zed is looking at me curiously. He looks a bit spooked, as a matter of fact. Of course, like all the kids I know, he's a little freaked out because he knows I see things.

Suddenly, I'm tired of it all. I'm tired of trying to appear normal. Tired of striving not to freak people out.

Especially to Zed. I didn't want to have to do that with him.

I want to say "boo!" But instead I just say "see ya," and take off.

It's an easy ride past Hassam's to the development. The farm stand is open, and Mr. Hassam waves as I spin by. I turn the corner and ride toward the new road into the development, cruising past the evergreens and the fields.

The new development is a shock. It hasn't been landscaped yet, and the empty houses look naked on their dirt lots. Most of the houses on Beewick were built in the early part of the last century, and they've tried to follow that model, but they've blown up the farmhouses into huge monsters with oversize windows and double doors. Their garages are thrust forward. I imagine all those garage doors open, and it would be like gaping mouths facing the streets, ready to chomp on anyone strolling by.

I can see signs of vandalism. One garage is splattered with red paint. Another one's yard is littered with refuse.

It's easy to find the house that Zed was talking

about. It's at the end of Larch Lane, and it's the only one on that road with full access to the bay. I bump my bike over the dirt and walk it, avoiding the trash in the front yard. I park it behind the house.

This house has a private dock at the bottom of a hill that leads down from the back deck. One day, this will be a lawn. One day, I guess, it will be beautiful, but I just don't have the imagination to see it.

I prowl around the house, peeking in the windows. Everything is shut tight. One window is boarded up, so I guess it had been smashed in the break-in. The house is totally empty inside. There's nothing to see. I start to wonder why I came. There are no clues here. There is nothing to pick up on.

I sit down on the steps of the back deck. There's a bag crumpled up underneath, shoved down behind the stairs. I reach down and pick it up. Just garbage, a bag from Starbucks with two empty coffee cups inside. I look at the sides of the cups, where they mark them. One was a cappuccino. The other was a tall nonfat latte, double shot. The bag feels heavy, which is weird, because the cups are empty. I feel a wave of sadness that makes no sense.

And then I feel it. A shudder inside me. The bag feels warm and heavy, as if the coffee cups are full.

Surprise floods me. But it isn't my surprise. I am feeling *someone else's* surprise. I hear a different heartbeat thud in my ears, hammering in panic.

The shock of the cold water takes my breath away. My head, my head . . .

I flail, while fireworks explode behind my eyes.

My heart is going to burst inside my chest. It is going to bloom like a rose.

It's him. It's Hank Hobbs. I can feel him, see him.

And someone is watching him drown.

And that someone feels nothing but impatience. No panic. No sorrow.

I hear footsteps against gravel.

Gravel?

I open my eyes. I am on the deck again. I am covered in sweat.

And the footsteps are real.

ELEVEN

I must be truly spooked in general, because I'm ready to pick up a stray beam and swing it at whoever appears. So it's kind of good that I don't, considering that Jeff Ferris appears with his father. They're both wearing suits, but they've tucked their pants into knee-high rubber boots. The sight of that is so silly that my fear drains away immediately. Anyway, since Jeff still owns the house, it makes perfect sense that he would be visiting it.

The reason for my presence, on the other hand, is not so clear.

"Gracie Kenzie," Jeff says. "What are you doing out here?"

"I hear so much about these houses," I say. "I just wanted to see for myself how great they are."

"Yeah. Look at that view." Jeff turns toward the cove and clicks into realtor mode. "It's one of the prime spots on the island."

His dad's gaze roams over the back of the house. "Looks all right. We'd better check the inside, though. Kids. That Fusilli should throw them in jail."

"He doesn't know who they are, Dad."

"Are you going to move in here?" I ask.

Jeff shakes his head. "I bought it for an investment, but man, it hurts to let it go."

"They vandalized our office," Franklin Ferris says. "They turned off the refrigerator so everything would spoil. Somebody smeared peanut butter all over my desk. I'm allergic to peanut butter! What kind of a person would do something like that?"

I just catch a hint of a smile as Jeff bends down to knock some dirt off the rubber boots he's wearing. Could it be that Jeff is amused at the thought of his prissy father getting hives? He slides a look at me. "You know Mason Patterson, right?"

"My cousin goes out with his sister, so yeah, I guess so."

"He's a good kid," Jeff says neutrally. He doesn't fool me. He's wondering if I'm in with the crowd who's vandalizing the development. So is his dad, who clears his throat and looks away. "So. How's the house?"

"Still standing. Did you hear about Hank Hobbs?"

Jeff nods. "Freaky, huh? My loss — he'd just gone to contract on this house. I had lunch with him right before he died. I mean, I guess I did. They found him the next day."

"I don't know why," Franklin Ferris says, "everywhere I go, I have to discuss this."

"Dad sold Hobbs his first house on Beewick. A big sale for us, back then."

"Did he seem depressed or weird or anything?" I ask Jeff.

"No. Why? Do they think he committed suicide?"

"They don't know."

"Well, neither do I. He seemed fine. But you never know what's in someone's head."

Jeff doesn't look too thrilled at discussing a former client with a teenager. I have a feeling I'm at the end of my conversational rope with him. His dad has decided to ignore me. He's wandering over to look in the windows.

We hear the noise of a car door slamming. Footsteps head toward us. This time I'm not scared. I have a feeling I know who it is.

Joe Fusilli heads toward us. He steps in an enormous mud puddle on the way, which really pisses him off. He should have worn a pair of rubber boots. He shakes off some of the mud and keeps on coming.

"Gracie. What are you doing out here?"

"Checking out the view," I say.

He gives me that Joe-probe, the look that's supposed to make me squirm, but I don't react, so he turns to Jeff and his father. "Hi, Jeff, Franklin. Glad I ran into you — I left a message on your cell. I wanted to look around a bit."

"Sure. No problem."

Joe notices that I'm still holding the Starbucks bag. "What's that?"

"I found it here," I say, pointing to the stairs. "I think Hank Hobbs left it here."

"Why do you say that?" Joe asks.

I shrug. Joe sighs.

He whips out a pair of latex gloves from his pocket and takes the bag from me. He lifts out first one cup, then the other. He bends down to look. "Lipstick stain," he says.

He turns to Jeff. "Did Hobbs come here with his wife?"

Jeff looks uncomfortable. "You know, a realtor is like a psychiatrist, in a way. We know everybody's secrets."

"Like who's getting divorced?"

Jeff shoves his hands in his pockets. "I heard him talking to a Betsy on the phone. His wife's name is Pam."

"Jeff, that's gossip," Franklin Ferris says disapprovingly.

"Actually, it's not," Joe says. "I'm investigating a death. Go on, Jeff."

"I was struck by the conversation, because I thought he was talking to his wife. He had that tone in his voice. And whenever we talked about this house, he never mentioned her. So I just kind of assumed that maybe," Jeff looks at his father nervously, "there was someone else. But of course I don't know anything for sure."

Joe is writing in his notepad. "There's no Starbucks on the island," he says. "Whoever this Betsy is, she could be from the mainland."

"Well, Hank Hobbs lived in Seattle," Jeff says. "I mean, you know that, of course. I'm just trying to be helpful."

Joe puts the cups and the bag into a plastic bag and seals it. "Can you show me around?" he asks Jeff.

"Sure."

Nobody pays attention to me, so I tag behind them as Jeff opens the door and punches a code into the keypad to turn off the alarm.

"Never thought I'd have to use an alarm on Beewick," Jeff says. "That's a sad thing."

"We sold houses with alarms twenty years ago," Franklin Ferris says. "I hate this false sentimentality."

"These days, we have to remember so many codes and passwords, it's a wonder our heads don't explode," Joe says as he pokes around the empty kitchen. "My secret system is to code everything on my dog's birthday."

"You remember your dog's birthday?" Jeff asks, amused.

"No. That's the problem," Joe says, bending down to open the cabinet under the sink.

"Ha," Jeff chortles appreciatively.

We follow Joe around the house. I can tell he's disappointed by the lack of clues. The house is not only empty, it's clean. There are amazing views from all the bedrooms, and each bedroom has its own bathroom. That would sure cut down on arguments in Shay's house, let me tell you.

"Let's take a look at the dock," Joe says when he's finished.

"I was hoping we could get back to town," Franklin Ferris says.

"Just another few minutes," Joe says. It's clear they can't say no.

Franklin Ferris's face is flushed as we walk out the door. He doesn't like being told what to do, that's for sure.

I'm keeping very quiet, hoping they'll just forget I'm there. Nobody suggests it's time for me to get lost, so I trail behind them down the incline to the dock. Jeff punches another keypad, and the gate swings open. Our footsteps thud along the wooden dock as we walk down toward the end.

Joe stops at the pilings and runs his fingers along one. "Someone tied up a boat here."

"I'm not surprised," Jeff says. "Folks like to come into this cove to fish. Some of them probably use the dock, even though they're not supposed to."

"Did Hobbs ever come to the house by water?" Joe asks.

"He never mentioned it."

Suddenly, I notice Joe's body stiffen. He's seen something. He squats and plucks something that had been wedged into the dock boards. He holds it up. It's a small capsule.

"Vitamin?" Jeff asks.

Joe slips it into a ziplock bag. "We'll see."

Joe looks around some more, but the light is fading. Franklin Ferris looks at his watch in an obvious way.

"Well, I guess it's time to shove off. Thanks for your time," Joe says. "Gracie, I'll give you a ride home. We'll throw your bike in the trunk."

We walk back down the dock and up the hill to the house, then tromp through the mud back to the driveway. Joe looks mournfully at the state of his shoes. While Joe puts my bike in the trunk, I watch as Jeff and his dad sit in his car with the doors open. Together, they take off their rubber boots and put on their shoes. Jeff takes the boots and puts them in the trunk. He waves as he drives off. Franklin Ferris stares straight ahead.

I slide into the front seat. Joe just drives for a while.

As he hits the main road back toward Shay's, he nods a couple of times, as if to give himself courage.

"I spoke to your dad."

Somehow I don't like hearing the word *dad* associated with him. "Nate," I say.

"I think I scared him when I showed up. He seemed to want to defend himself from me, as if I was going to arrest him for being a deadbeat dad. I could have. I wanted to."

I have to admit I get some pleasure out of that.

"I didn't think that's what you or Shay would want."

"No. I don't want him in jail. Mom never cared about the child support payments. She was lucky she didn't have to. She just divorced him and never tried to find him."

"I just want you to know that I'll do whatever I can for you, Gracie. That's all. That includes running him out of town if you want me to."

Well, here it is. I could make him disappear. All I have to do is say a word.

"That's okay," I say.

"There's nothing wrong with spending a bit of time with him, and then sending him on his way."

I twist in my seat to face Joe. His expression is stern as he drives. "You don't like him," I say.

"Men who abandon their children are the worst sort."

"He was sick. He thought we were better off without him."

Joe's mouth twists. "They all say that, honey."

"Is he a suspect?"

"Well, he didn't know Hank Hobbs. Never met him, he said. Shay backed him up."

You might think Joe is finished, but I know something else is coming. He pulls into my driveway.

"Are you coming in?" I ask. "I'm sure Shay wants to see you. Even if she's still mad at you."

He shakes his head. "Stay out of the Hobbs case," he says.

"I *am* out of it."

"I mean it, Gracie," Joe says. "Don't forget what happened last time. You started poking around, and the next thing you knew, you were kidnapped by a seriously disturbed guy. We're talking about a murderer here."

"But you don't know Hank Hobbs was murdered for sure."

"I know he was."

"You got the autopsy reports?"

"He was smashed on the head and pushed into that water when he was still alive," Joe says. "Whoever did it is dangerous. Are you getting this now?"

"It's just hard," I say, "when I see things . . ."

"What do you see?"

I shake my head. "Nothing that would help you."

I get out of the car and lean in the open door for a minute. "Thanks for looking out for me," I say.

"Just doing my job," Joe tells me. "Now do yours. Be a kid. Not a detective."

Once I get my bike from his trunk, he pulls out

and drives away. The evergreens look black, with spiky tips brushing the darkening sky. I shiver, thinking of what I saw. I had stood behind a killer's eyes and watched him kill.

I wish I could stay out of it. I wish I could. I wish I could turn off the visions.

If only.

TWELVE

After my mom was killed, after I got over the shock of it, I discovered parts of me I wish I hadn't. I didn't know I had it in me to be mean. I didn't know that I could turn away from someone trying to help me, and not even care. I didn't know I was capable of so much anger at the world.

I look back on that time, when I shut the door in my grandmother's face, when I told my best friend in Maryland that she was stupid, when I hated Shay whenever she smiled or laughed, hated her for breathing when her sister was dead. . . . Well. I'm just grateful that everyone forgave me.

Of course my friend Jessie back in Maryland may have forgiven me, but our friendship will never be the same. Still, I'm grateful to her for trying. Grateful to her for sending me e-mails, photographs of the friends I used to have, so I don't feel completely lost in the world.

A river of pain still cuts a path through me. Sometimes I get pulled under. When the people who love me say "it's okay," I feel lucky.

I stare down at the thirteen birthday cards I've laid out on my bed.

I get that my father did a very bad thing. But part of me remembers that time in my own life, and part of me wonders: When everyone has forgiven me, why can't I take even one tiny step toward forgiving him?

He waits for me again after school. Hands in the pockets of his jacket, looking like another teacher, a new history teacher who all the girls have secret crushes on. I notice how the other students are trying not to watch as I come up and we fall into step together.

There is no problem with rhythm. Even though his legs are long, he matches my stride. I look down at us, our legs, both in jeans, walking. Is there a secret rhythm that fathers and daughters have, no matter what?

"Want me to carry your backpack?"

"I've managed to do it myself since I was seven."

He breathes in and out. "I just have to make a personal observation," he says. "When you've screwed up as badly as I have, there's about a million minefields in every ordinary conversation. And I keep triggering every single one. Pow."

"I've noticed that," I say.

"Do you admire me at least for trying?"

"Actually, no."

"Pow. There goes another one."

We're quiet for a while, but it's a better silence.

"I thought I'd leave," Nate says. "I think it's better for now. You have my address and phone numbers and e-mail. Can I write you once in a while?"

"I guess so."

"Gracie." Nate stops, so I stop, too. On him, my unruly hair makes sense. He looks so ordinary, a handsome guy who's just a little careworn, who's seen a little too much sun and hard times. I see that his eyes aren't quite as dark as mine. They aren't the same color, after all. I note a thousand details of his face in one small moment, and the living reality of him makes me feel disoriented, as though I'd made him up and he suddenly appeared. "What I would really, really like is to take you to dinner tonight."

Everything I've been thinking, everything I've been feeling, tugs me into different directions. But there is one through line: I'm hungry to know him. If he leaves tomorrow and I don't do this, I'll regret it.

He sees the answer on my face, and he smiles.

"It occurs to me that I didn't tell you that I loved your mother," Nate says. "I should say those words out loud. Just because they hurt doesn't mean I shouldn't say them. I let her down so badly. But she was the love of my life."

We're sitting in the restaurant that's in the Greystone Inn. We have a quiet table against a wall. Candles are lit. The potato-leek soup was awesome. My dad is nursing a glass of wine. We both have ordered the lasagna.

Just a father-daughter dinner.

"It was love at first sight," Nate says. "That old corny thing. I was about to back out of the deal to buy the house with Shay, to tell you the truth. I don't know why I agreed to go in on it in the first place. I inherited some money from my aunt, and I was afraid if I didn't invest it, I'd blow it, I guess. I was regretting it until Carrie walked through the door. I even remember what she was wearing, that sweater . . . the color of cornflowers."

He isn't here anymore. He's back in the past. His eyes suddenly have a light in them.

"What was it like, that summer?" I ask.

"Crazy fun. I have to admit, I went to Beewick because it would be free. The group back in Seattle was picking up expenses, and we were camping out in summer. We'd swim at midnight — man, it was cold. I'm not much of a swimmer, so splashing around made sense, just to keep warm. We had some wicked softball games. One night, I crashed a big society party at the country club. One of the locals sneaked me in. It was all such a blast. And then it all went bad. Billy disappeared, and we were all worried about him. Shay thought Hobbs had done something to him, but I thought it was more likely that Hobbs paid him off. Billy hated his family — I wouldn't blame him for disappearing."

"You think that's a solution? Disappearing?"

He comes back to the present and looks at me across the table. He doesn't flinch. "Honey, I didn't hate you. I didn't hate your mom. Sometimes you leave because you love your family so much. You don't want to keep hurting them."

I push my food around, not answering. It's not enough, and he knows it.

"Ohh-kay, maybe I should stick with the past. Shay just couldn't believe that Billy would run out on her without a word. She was in love with him, after all."

"Shay was in love with Billy?"

"Well, sure. They were a couple. They came up to Beewick together. Then she broke up with him, and he was destroyed. I guess Billy thought he didn't have anything to lose, confronting Hobbs."

This was news to me. Shay had never mentioned being in love with Billy. What else was she concealing?

Nate doesn't notice my surprise.

"Did you ever meet Hank Hobbs?" I ask him.

He shakes his head. "We were fighting this abstraction — the Big Evil Corporation. We didn't know any of the executives. Billy was the one who found out somehow that Hank Hobbs was leading the cover-up — or that's what he thought, anyway. Then, for a brief period, Shay herself was under suspicion," he says. "That's why Carrie came out. It wasn't just to help with the house. She wanted to protect Shay. When Carrie and I fell in love, Shay wasn't crazy about it. I guessed at the time that she had feelings for me. She was upset about Billy, maybe she was looking for something to help her . . . maybe she wanted something to happen with us, and I fell for her sister instead." Nate shrugs. "She didn't come to the wedding. Carrie was devastated. They were very close, and Shay's disapproval really hurt her."

"Of course," I point out, "it turned out that Shay was right."

"Yeah, that's the irony, isn't it? Shay was right. Maybe I suspected that she was, even then. I never felt good enough for Carrie."

"You *weren't* good enough for her."

"Believe me, muffin, I know."

He keeps talking, but I'm not there anymore. The word *muffin* spirals me out, away from the table, into a past. His past. Or is it his present? His future?

The light is so bright, summer light. I see him handing something to a little girl, a stuffed rabbit. "There you go, muffin," he says. "Good as new."

The girl is blond and wearing a white dress. I am her negative image. I am a dark spot and she is shining light.

When I return to the now, he's talking, and I

struggle to focus. "I'm betting that Shay wasn't devastated when I left. I'm sure she thought you two were better off. I'm not good enough for Rachel, either. I'm just lucky she sticks around." Nate grins. "The woman loves a project."

He leans over the table. "I look at you, my beautiful daughter, and I think — everything you are is perfect."

I'm not about to buy that. I'm still thinking of the pale little girl. "You don't even know me."

"But I know it's true. I want you to know that I told Shay that I'm signing over my half of the house to her as long as you can inherit it."

I guess I'm supposed to gasp and say thanks. But it means so little to me. Half a house? Is that payback? Is that what it's all worth to him?

I think he realizes what I'm thinking, because he leans back, and suddenly, it's like, pull up a chair, because sadness just walked in the door.

There isn't anything he can say, anything he can give me, that will make up for not having him. He knows it. I know it.

I just don't know what to do with it.

Nate drives me home. I get out. He gets out. I wonder if we're supposed to hug when we say good-bye, and if I want us to.

But suddenly, a shadow moves across the lawn and forms into a person, rushing at us, and I gasp.

It's Mason. He looks bigger in the dark.

Nate moves in front of me so quickly, I don't have time to think.

Mason points a finger at me. "Stay out of my business, Kenzie, or you'll be sorry!"

"What are you talking about?" I ask. "I'm not in your business."

"Just keep your freaky nose out of it, freak!"

"Hey!" Nate moves smoothly forward and puts his hand on Mason's shoulder. He must have applied a nice amount of pressure, because Mason steps back as though he's propelled.

"Good night, friend," Nate says. "That's enough."

Mason shoots me a dirty look as he goes.

"What was he talking about?" Nate asks.

"I don't know."

"Do you want me to stick around?"

What a question. Another wrong step in the minefield. Of course I want him to stick around. I've wanted him to stick around since I was three years old.

I say what I always told myself on all those days I missed him, on all those times I wondered about him, on all those nights I dreamed of him.

"I'll be fine."

THIRTEEN

The next day, we have off for a teachers' conference, which is a gift. I don't want to have to face Mason at school. I don't know why he's angry at me, but I'm sure it has something to do with Hank Hobbs.

I'm still spooked to be in the house, but I decide to be brave and hit Diego's computer after he leaves for work.

I plug *Hank Hobbs* into a search engine. Even Joe couldn't be angry with me about that. I can't believe the flood of information that comes up. He had some career going, and he was on the boards of a bunch of companies. It makes for rough going. I can't get through the information overload, and after spending over an hour scrolling through corporate newsletters and articles about "synergistic strategies," I feel like my brain cells are going to fuse.

Time for my own personal computer geek.

I met Ryan last summer, when I was nosing around trying to find out what had happened to Emily. He had a bit of a crush on her, and a bit of a crush on me, but now he has a girlfriend, Tobie, so we're able to be friends. Whenever I have a glitch I can't solve, I call Ryan, and he leads me through a fix-it strategy while blasting my ear with his newest obsessions — last time it was polka-rock (yes, really), the mating habits of polar bears, and Turkish food.

"Gracie! Awesome!" Ryan also has a tendency to speak in exclamation points. "What brings you to call me on my landline?"

"I've got a sleuthing problem."

"Talk on, Nancy Drew."

I explain my information deluge, and what I'm looking for.

"No worries!" Ryan says. "I can devise the right string to find the info. Can you hang on for a few?"

I hang on. I hear the clackety-clack of computer keys.

"Got something!" Ryan says. "Hang on. . . . Yeah, the newspaper on Beewick back there in the ice age was called the *Beacon,* not the *Star.* And they totally rock, because their archives are all online. Some sort of historical record project. I'm going to e-mail this to you."

A moment later, Ryan's e-mail pops up. I click on the URL.

"ACCUSATIONS LEVELED AT MONVOR FOLLOWING DISAPPEARANCE"

I read the article quickly. Shay is quoted saying that Billy Applegate went off to see Hank Hobbs. She makes it clear that she suspects him of hiding something and challenges him in print to "tell the truth about what happened that night."

No wonder Hank Hobbs tried to get her fired.

At the end of the article, it notes, "Ms. Kenzie has also been questioned regarding Mr. Applegate's disappearance."

So Nate was right.

"Here's something interesting," Ryan says, breaking into my thoughts.

My little flag pops up, and I click on Ryan's e-mail. He's included a paragraph from another article that mentions that Hank Hobbs's house was broken into twenty years ago. The police investigated and "concluded that it has no connection to the Applegate disappearance." A few things were stolen, including a briefcase. "I was certain I'd set the alarm, but I guess I didn't," Hobbs said.

A briefcase was stolen. Could it have contained the documents that Billy Applegate had claimed to have, the ones that proved that Monvor had falsified data? The break-in had happened just a few days before he disappeared. Just around the time he told the group that he had the goods on Monvor.

"It's got to be it," I whisper.

"Hey, this is weird," Ryan says. "This guy Hobbs was married to a woman named Pam. But back then, he got engaged to someone else."

"Who?"

"An Elizabeth Anne Dunwoody. I love these

announcements, they are so *incredibly* cornball. Elizabeth, known as Betsy, has attended the Heath School in Seattle and is currently —"

"Known as Betsy!" Jeff Ferris had heard Hank talking to a Betsy on the phone.

"Is that something? Did I find something?"

"You are an incredible genius."

"I have to inform you, Gracie, that I am taken. Tobie is the axis around which I revolve. So even though I worship your completely awesome personhood, we must remain attached on only a spiritual plane —"

"Can you find out if Betsy Dunwoody is still living around here?"

"Does a chicken have lips?" I hear keys clacking again. "Betsy Dunwoody married someone else. She is now Mrs. Elizabeth Dunwoody Wheeler, and she lives in Bellevue, Washington. Let me see . . . museum trustee, country club, chair of Save the Parklands committee . . . yeah, we're talking major Betsy bucks."

Bellevue is a swanky suburb of Seattle. It's only an hour south of here. And Diego has a car.

FOURTEEN

"You're kidding, right? Because if you're not kidding, you're nuts." Diego sits at the kitchen table, his spoon halfway to his mouth. He'd just been about to dive into a tempting bowl of Shay's granola. I like to hit him up in the mornings, before he's made plans. Marigold sleeps late on Saturdays, but Diego is an early riser. He always wakes up in a good mood, too.

That is, if I don't spoil it.

By my silence Diego correctly assumes that I'm not kidding.

"You're nuts," he says again. "Do you happen to remember what happened the last time I drove you into Seattle on the trail of a kidnapper? And do you happen to remember that you yourself were kidnapped while I stood around in the park half out of my mind? Do you remember that my mother has still never forgiven me?"

"All of this is true," I say. "But this is different. I'm not investigating a suspect. I just want to talk to —"

"That's what you said last time!"

It's clear I have to tell Diego everything. I pull

out a chair and sit down. "Joe thinks Shay is a suspect in the murder of Hank Hobbs," I say.

"That's ridiculous."

"Of course it is. He also thinks it might have been my father."

Diego blinks. "Not so ridiculous," he says. "I mean, he just shows up on the same weekend that someone is found dead. . . ."

"Yeah. Exactly. So I'm going to go from the weird girl who sees things to the weird girl who sees things whose father is a murderer. Can't wait."

"It doesn't matter what your father is, or does. Anyone who knows you knows —"

"Diego, you sound like a guidance counselor. Come on."

"Well, it's true. I never knew my father. He could be a murderer."

"But he isn't, is he?"

Diego takes a sip of juice. His father is something we never talk about in this house. Nineteen years ago, Shay went on a trip to Spain and came back pregnant. She simply told her family that she was having the baby and raising it, and his father would never be discussed. Somehow, she pulled it off.

I've asked Diego about his father. He's told me that he knows some things, but it's obviously difficult for Shay to talk about, so he doesn't ask her about it. And when I press him for details, he fixes me with his beautiful liquid eyes and tells me to ask Shay.

I still haven't worked up the nerve.

"My granola's getting soggy," Diego says.

"So's your logic. And if those two candidates for the slammer aren't enough, the other suspect is Mason Patterson. Do you want Marigold's brother to go to jail?"

Diego doesn't say anything. He's thinking.

"This woman was engaged to Hank Hobbs twenty years ago. Maybe they reconnected. Maybe she knows something. Maybe if we just go down there and talk to her, we'll be able to go to Joe and give him a new suspect. Just think how grateful Marigold would be if you took the heat off Mason. You'd be the man."

"When you start talking like a bad TV show, I know you're desperate," Diego says. "I don't care about being a hero to Marigold. I just want to bask in her lovelight."

"Oh, gross!"

Diego grins. "But I'll take you."

Diego may give me a hard time, but secretly, he loves surveillance. We sat outside Betsy Dunwoody Wheeler's McMansion in Bellevue in Diego's old Saab, watching the house.

"What if she doesn't come out?"

"It's Saturday morning. Everybody goes out on Saturday morning sometime."

"Wait, I see the side door opening —"

"It's her! Duck!"

"Why?" Diego asks me. "She doesn't know us."

"Oh. Right." I peer through the windshield as Betsy gets into a Mercedes SUV.

"Looking good for a mom," Diego notes approvingly.

It's true. Betsy has a trim body, and her chin-length blond hair is glossy and full. From behind, you could mistake her for a teenager, especially for the jeans and tiny jacket she wears. She starts the car and drives down the long driveway toward us.

She turns into the street and we follow, winding through the neighborhood and then out onto the main road. When she turns at the light, we turn. When she picks up speed, we pick up speed.

"You're loving this, aren't you?" I say to Diego.

"Don't push it," he says.

Suddenly, Betsy pulls over.

"She's going to that Starbucks!" I yell. "Pull over!"

"Why, do you want a latte?"

Betsy gets out of the car and goes into Starbucks.

"Wait here," I say to Diego.

"Bring me a cookie!" Diego yells after me as I scoot out.

I follow Betsy into the Starbucks. I maneuver close to her, pretending to study the muffin selection.

"A tall two-shot nonfat latte," Betsy says.

Bingo.

I race back to the car.

"Where's my cookie?"

"She ordered a double-shot nonfat latte," I say. "Just like the cup on Beewick. That was definitely her!"

"What now?" Diego asks. "Should we go in and talk to her?"

I shake my head. "She's leaving. We have to keep following her."

Diego pulls out after Betsy. We follow her through the hills, up and down the twisting roads, trying to keep at least one car behind her. Finally, she pulls into the long, curving drive of the Conifer Country Club.

We drive in. Diego parks the car an aisle away from her.

"We're going to have to talk to her quickly," he says. "We can get busted if we don't. We're not members."

It occurs to me at this moment that I have no idea what I'm going to say. But it's too late now. I get out of the car and we walk toward Betsy. She's grabbed a tote bag and is heading for the front door of the club, swinging the bag as she walks. She reaches the front door before we can catch up and disappears inside.

"Now or never," Diego says.

I push open the door. My foot hits a deep rug on a bleached wood floor. A huge orange glass object is spotlit on a shelf, looking like a giant clam. I see paintings. What Shay would call window treatments, not curtains. The whole place screams "tasteful."

"Go," Diego says. He gives me a small push in the middle of my back.

I need it. I'm intimidated.

"Betsy!" I cry. My voice sounds like a croak.

I try again. "Betsy?"

She hears me this time. She turns, already smiling, thinking I'm a daughter of a friend, perhaps. I see her searching her memory banks.

So I blurt out the thing I shouldn't say, the only thing I can say.

"Isn't it sad about Hank Hobbs?"

Her smile disappears. I see panic in her eyes now. And the panic opens her up to me like a picture book.

I see . . . a small, empty room with a raised platform and a view outside to the tops of trees. Skylight overhead. I hear a woman crying.

. . . a white carnation, its petals brown and crumbling.

. . . an ache somewhere, something hurting, a knee.

"Yes. I haven't seen him in years, though." She backs away a step and then the smile is there again, a practiced smile.

"That's not exactly true," I say.

Her eyes flick from me to Diego, and suddenly, she looks hard. "Who are you?"

"We live on Beewick Island," I say. "We —"

"I don't know you."

"We just wanted to ask you a few questions," Diego says. "That's all. We're not here to harass you." He smiles at her in a friendly way.

Usually, when Diego turns on his charm to any female with a pulse, he gets results. But not with Betsy.

"You're not members here, are you?" she says in a glacial tone. Her gaze roams the hallway behind us. "I'll find someone to escort you back to the parking lot."

"How's your knee?" I ask.

"My knee?" She looks confused again.

"I know it's still bothering you."

"An old ski injury. How do . . ."

"And that room you built at the top of your house, where you go to be alone . . . you were going to do yoga there, but all you do is cry. Alone. Where no one can hear you."

"H-h-how do you know these things?"

"You wonder if your whole life is a mistake, but then you look at your children and you think, *How could I think that?* But you keep thinking it."

"Who are you?" she whispers.

"The carnation that means so much to you . . ."

Now she gives a cry and steps back, her hand at her throat.

Diego puts a hand under her elbow. There's a fireplace at one end of the long hallway, with some armchairs around it. He walks her all the way there, gently places her in one, then draws the others closer. We sit.

"What is this?" Betsy asks. "What's going on? Who *are* you?"

"My cousin is a psychic," Diego says. "She sees things."

"And you were drawn to me for some reason?" Betsy's green eyes are wide. I can tell that this excites her. Betsy's not a skeptic. She's eager to believe.

"Yes." I pitch my voice low, trying to sound more mature, like someone she'd listen to . . . and give answers to. "Hank's death left disturbances behind."

"Oh." The word is a cry, and Betsy presses her hand against her heart. "It did."

"You loved Hank Hobbs," I say, because I'm picking this up most of all. "You met him on

Beewick Island. You saw his new house, the house he was buying so that you could be together."

She bites her lower lip and looks up at me. "How did you know about the carnation?"

"The carnation?" Diego asks.

I nod to give Betsy encouragement. I know what I saw, but I don't know why I saw it, or what it means to her.

"It was . . . a joke," Betsy says. "From one afternoon when Hank and I were together . . . after he found me again. He couldn't remember my favorite flowers, and I teased him, because he remembered everything else. The day we met. The song that was playing the night we got engaged. What I wore, the things I said . . . it was amazing. So I reminded him that I didn't have a favorite flower, but the only flower I couldn't stand was a carnation. That night, when I got home, I opened my purse . . . and there was a carnation." She smiled. "I don't know how he found one and sneaked it in there, but he made me laugh. That was the day I knew I still loved him."

"So he looked you up," I say.

"It had been so long. Twenty years. And he e-mailed me out of the blue — *Are you the Betsy Dunwoody with eyes the color of sea glass?* We started writing, and then we met, and then . . ." She looked at the fire. "We didn't have an affair. We just wanted to be friends. We didn't want to fall in love." She looks down at the rings on her left hand, a band with three large diamonds, and, above it, a square-shaped diamond.

"You were thinking of leaving your husband."

"Yes," she whispers. "How do you know these things? Do you . . . see things in me? Things you want to tell me? Because there is so much I want to know."

I see bottomless need in her eyes. Here is a woman in need of so many things — reassurance, direction. I don't really have any for her. I can't tell her about her life. I can't tell her if she made the right choices. She doesn't understand that even though I can pick up flashes from her, I can't validate her. But that's what she wants.

I'm not sure what to do. I search in my mind for the right tone, the right words. And then I think of a role model. The person we look up to more than anyone, the person who spells it out for us, the person who asks the right questions in the right way.

Oprah.

"Tell me more about Hank," I say. "He seems to be a key for you."

She gives a sad smile. "A key to a different past. A past I should have had. I met him at a dance at the Beewick Club. I drove up to Beewick that weekend with some friends. There was a dance on Bastille Day. We were all dressed like French revolutionaries and royalty. It was silly, but we had fun. Hank just kept coming over to ask me to dance until my escort wanted to take him outside. I didn't care. I left with Hank. He drove me all the way home that night — all the way back to Seattle. A month later, he asked me to marry him. I didn't have one single doubt. And then . . ."

"And then?" Diego asks.

"There was that business with the missing young man."

"Billy Applegate."

"Was that his name? I don't remember. It was all so ridiculous — of course Hank didn't have anything to do with it. But some horrible woman accused him."

Diego and I exchange a look. That was Shay.

"His name got in the papers. And then apparently, there were some other things about his company, what they were doing on Beewick . . ."

"Polluting it," Diego says.

"Well, that's what they said. Hank didn't have anything to do with that, either — he was just a vice president." Betsy pushes at her hair, managing to brush it out of her eyes without ruffling it. "But with my parents, you just don't get your name in the papers. Once when you're married, once when you die, but that's it. My dad played golf with the chairman of the board of Monvor, and the chairman hinted that maybe Hank would lose his job. The chairman said he was careless — but Hank was the most careful man! He had enemies at that company. But my parents didn't understand. They never liked Hank anyway, and they were totally against the engagement, so they started pressuring me."

Betsy looks at the fire again. "It was so hard for me. I didn't know what to do. I was young, only twenty-one. Hank was more than ten years older than I was. . . . I was just a kid. I couldn't go against my parents. And Hank lived full-time on Beewick then. Nobody lived on Beewick. It's not like it is now. So my parents . . . they just thought, here's our daughter, marrying this guy, maybe he's a criminal, maybe he'll get fired, and he's taking her to this island in the middle of Puget Sound. So I broke it off."

Wow. Was this story for real?

Her hands twist in her lap. "Hank was so upset. He said I had to believe in him. That he was taking care of everything, that there was no way in the world they would fire him. But I didn't listen. I thought maybe my parents were right. Maybe my first love wasn't my real love." She looks up at us, tears swimming in her green eyes. "But it was. It was!"

"And he never got over you," I say.

"That's what he said. He wanted to leave his wife and start over, start living the life he said he was meant to live. And now he can't. And neither can I." Betsy ends on a sob. A couple passing by looks over, but Diego's stare tells them to butt out.

She lifts her head from her hands. Mascara has smudged underneath her eyes. "Can you tell me how he is?" she whispers. "You can feel him still, can't you? Can you tell him I'm sorry for what I did?"

"Sorry?" I repeat. My heartbeat quickens. What will Betsy reveal?

"I should have told him that last day I would go with him. We drove up together and he showed me that house and said he was buying it for me. He laid out his whole life, his whole plan on how we would live, where we would travel. . . . And I could see it. But I didn't tell him yes. I told him I needed more time. But I would have gone with him! Can you tell him that?"

"I'm not in touch with Hank," I say. "But I feel he knew that you loved him."

Diego nudges me with his foot. He knows I'm giving her a line. But it's not just that I want more information. I want to make her feel better.

"Betsy, did you know Nathaniel Millard?" I ask. I know time is running out. In another minute, Betsy will come to herself and realize she's unburdening herself of memories to two strangers. She'll feel uncomfortable, and she'll split.

She looks blank and shakes her head.

"Shay Kenzie?"

"No idea."

"They spent the summer on Beewick twenty years ago, along with Billy Applegate."

"I only went to Beewick one time back then," she says. "The night I met Hank. Hank always came to Seattle to see me. He drove in every weekend, and it wasn't as fast a trip then, either. He was so devoted. And I never, never truly appreciated it. And now I've lost him!"

Now Diego rolls his eyes when Betsy isn't looking. I agree with him — there's sincerity in what Betsy is saying, but also just a little too much drama.

She looks at Diego. "Would you mind? Can I . . . talk to her alone?"

"Of course." Diego rises and drifts off. He pretends to study a case full of medals and trophies against one wall.

"Can you tell me anything else?" she asks me. "Anything I should know about me?"

Huh? Betsy is looking at me hungrily. I have to come up with something. "Keep up with the yoga," I say.

She nods, as though this is precious information. "And what about my husband? Should I leave him?"

What a question. How would I know?

I wonder what a psychic would say.

"You must move through your grief for Hank," I improvise. "Grief distorts your intention. Only when you move on can you see your path."

She nods again. "Thank you. Thank you."

She wipes at her eyes carefully, then gathers up her things and walks down the hall. I wander over to Diego.

"That was a bust," I say. "Hank was planning on leaving his wife, though. Joe should know that."

"He should know this, too," Diego says. He points to the wall. Betsy Wheeler has won the gold medal in her age class in every swim meet since the year 2000.

The significance clicks in.

"She could have swum to shore easily," I say.

FIFTEEN

Usually, Shay and Joe try to see each other three or four times a week, and Joe eats dinner at our house on Fridays. So I'm surprised when Shay suggests pizza night on Friday. She always likes to cook for Joe. She looks exhausted, and I suddenly realize that Joe hasn't exactly been burning up the phone lines, either.

"Joe's not coming?" I ask.

Shay has her back to me. She's getting out the phone book, even though pizza delivery is on speed dial. That's how addled she is.

"No, he's working," she says. I can't see her face, but I can see by her shoulders that she's sad. Or angry. Or both.

I wish I could see into my aunt's head. Normally, I don't have to. Shay is just out there. She tells you what's on her mind. I never get flashes about her, and I think it's not only because we're close, but because she's so clear, so direct. There is no secret engine driving her, the way it is with the others I can pick up things from.

Or so I thought. I never thought she could keep a secret from me, either.

Does everyone have a secret engine? I know what mine is — grief. The loss of my mother fuels me. What I want more than anything is for that grief to stop driving the bus.

What about Betsy Dunwoody? She's made a secret engine out of her confusion. She seems like an unlikely murder suspect, but I have to wonder if someone capable of that much ego and sadness could funnel it into rage. Could she have pushed Hank off that boat?

Shay seems unreachable right now, and that's weird. She's the one who keeps this house running, who keeps us together at the dinner table, who lights the fires, who cooks the meals, who looks up the weather every morning so she can tell us to wear our gloves. Even though she knows it drives Diego crazy to be told what to do like a kid.

Is it just the thing with Joe that's making her so withdrawn? Or is she worried about something else?

I know lots of things about Joe Fusilli, and one of the things I know is that every morning he goes to this bakery near his house and buys his mother a carrot muffin. She has Alzheimer's, and she lives with him. She has a caregiver who comes in during the day, and Joe's sister comes over on the nights Joe is out. It's hard on the family, but Joe is going to do it as long as he can, because that's the kind of guy he is.

Anyway, I don't know if Joe's mother remembers from one day to the next if she even likes carrot muffins, but he knows she does, and it makes her happy, so he buys a muffin and coffee for himself every morning at the BlueBay Diner. Which happens to be on my way to school.

I see his car parked in the lot, so I park my bike and walk in. Joe is sipping his coffee at the end of the counter, and an egg-white omelette sits in front of him. He's not really eating it. He looks as bummed as Shay.

"That's not much of a breakfast," I say, sliding onto the stool next to him. "Where's the toast?"

"I'm on a diet. Can I buy you something and watch you eat it? A muffin? Toast with butter? Chocolate cake?"

"No, thanks. I just stopped by when I saw your car. We haven't seen you."

"Yeah." Joe looks down into his coffee cup. "This case has me pretty busy."

"Did you and Shay have a fight?"

He puts the mug down on the counter. "No. Not really. But until this case is over, I have to watch out how things look."

"Because Shay is a suspect."

"Not to me, Gracie," Joe says. "Shay doesn't seem to get that." Sometimes his dark eyes seem to hold all the misery in the world. This is one of those times. "Of course I know that Shay couldn't have done anything like that — she doesn't have a homicidal bone in her body. But she does have motive, and she doesn't have an alibi for that evening. She was out at the wetlands site, alone."

"Oh. But she's probably really mad at you for asking her for an alibi."

"Let's say," Joe says, sipping his coffee, "it was not the most pleasant conversation."

"Well, I have something that might help you," I say. "A clue."

He raises his eyebrows at me. "This better involve a hunch, and nothing else. No more poking around."

"I found Betsy."

"You found Betsy."

"Betsy Dunwoody Wheeler. She was engaged to Hank Hobbs twenty years ago, and they were having an affair when he died. Well, she says they weren't, but I don't think she'd tell a couple of kids the truth, do you?"

"A couple of kids?"

Oops. I was supposed to leave Diego out of it. "Diego took me to see her." Joe's stare tells me to go on. "In Bellevue. We talked to her at the country club. And she's a champion swimmer, Joe! She could have whacked Hank with an oar or something, pushed him off the boat, waited for him to go down, and then swam back to shore, no problem."

Is that steam rising from the coffee, or is it coming out of Joe's ears?

"Gracie, I told you not to get involved."

"But what I did was, I —"

"I told you to stay out of this. It could be dangerous."

"I just thought if I talked to her, I could pick up something you couldn't."

Double oops. Definitely the wrong thing to say.

"I'm a trained *investigator*, Gracie."

"Right. And you are supreme. But I thought maybe I'd get a flash or two from her, and I did. Nothing about the murder. Just some other stuff that made her open up. She admitted that she'd been out to Beewick with him, Joe! And she had a double-shot latte —"

Joe groans and puts his head in his hands. "Stop." He pushes his coffee mug away and picks up the bag with the muffin in it. He stands up. "I will investigate Betsy Dunwoody Wheeler, and you will stay home and never — ever — do this again. I'm going to talk to Shay about this, Gracie. I mean it. Come on, I'll walk you out."

We walk out together. Joe is still fuming. I know he's mostly concerned about me getting myself into trouble again. What he doesn't realize is that I'm already in trouble. I'm already involved. Shay is a suspect. My father is a suspect. I can't just sit there and do nothing.

I have to know.

Joe pauses by my bike. "You going to school?"

I nod. Obviously, I'm going to school. Joe is leading up to something.

"Do me a favor. Don't start investigating Mason Patterson. Keep your distance, okay?"

"Why?"

"Just do it."

"But why?"

Joe sighs. He knows I'm not going to give up.

"We tested that capsule I found at the dock. It's andro."

"Andro?"

"Androstenedione. It's a steroid precursor popular among bodybuilders and athletes. We searched Mason's house last night and the identical brand was found in his room."

"So he was there. At Hank Hobbs's house."

"Could be. Could be he's involved somehow."

"Do you think he killed Hobbs?" I ask breathlessly.

"I don't know who killed Hobbs, and I don't discuss my cases with anyone," Joe says sternly. "The only reason I'm telling you this, Gracie, is that you might hear it at school today, and I don't want you asking Mason any questions. I want your nose out of it, do you hear me?"

"I'm out of it," I say. "I promise." And I mean it. Mostly because I don't want to cross Joe. But also because the last thing I want to do is tangle with Mason.

I'm hanging up my jacket in my locker when I see Marigold heading toward me. Sometimes she makes an effort to seek me out, but I think it's just to get points from Diego. Our conversations never really go anywhere, and I can tell she's relieved when she trills her "'bye now!"

But this morning is different.

This morning, Marigold finally gets real.

She is followed by her best friends, Ashley Hull and Kelly Farnsworth, and I suddenly get a sinking feeling. With teenage girls, the presence of a posse usually signals an ambush.

Marigold closes my locker door with a bang. "You've got a lot of nerve, Gracie Kenzie," she says.

I don't say anything, because I know there is no stopping her. Behind her, Kelly and Ashley glare at me.

"Stay away from my family," Marigold hisses. "I know you got Detective Fusilli to search our house. It was humiliating!"

"First of all, I had nothing to do with it," I say. "Second, didn't the police find something?"

Marigold's face flushes. "Mason is innocent! He doesn't take steroids! That was left there by somebody else. And now the police think he might have killed that guy!"

"Marigold, I have nothing to do with this," I say. "I don't know why you think I do."

"I know that your aunt dates Detective Fusilli. And I know you're a psychic weirdo," Marigold says. There are tears in her eyes. She's not just being mean. She's scared.

Scared of what?

That her brother will get arrested for something he didn't do? Or that he's guilty?

"You told the police that he was guilty," Marigold goes on.

"And Mason is totally innocent," Ashley Hull says. "He's the greatest guy, and now everyone will think he killed somebody."

I know that Ashley has a wicked crush on Mason. She seems particularly overheated.

"It is *so* irresponsible of you," Kelly says.

Kids are gathering around us. I want to open my locker and crawl back inside. I know that nothing I say to Marigold and her friends will make any difference. But I'm also angry at them for jumping to conclusions. For attacking me. I can feel my anger rush up from my feet to my head, and I feel words crowding my throat, things I shouldn't say.

"My mother won't come out of her room," Marigold says. "We had to hire a lawyer and everything, thanks to you. And I know why you did it, too. Diego told me."

My stomach drops to the floor, and I feel sick. "What did Diego tell you?"

"That your long-lost father is in town. That he suddenly shows up, and Hank Hobbs is dead. You don't want your dad to be a murderer, so you point the finger at my brother!"

Everything balls up inside me. Fear and anger and, most of all, loneliness. I have never felt so alone.

Except for one person. One person I never expected to think was on my side.

My dad.

Hearing someone else attack him does something to me. I feel blind rage, something black and ancient roars up from inside me.

"Marigold, I know it's hard for you to concentrate, especially in school," I say. "But make an effort. Get those brain cells to cooperate. I didn't say anything to Joe about Mason. If he's in trouble, it has nothing to do with me."

Marigold takes a breath. I see all the angry words bottled up in her, too, and now they come rushing out. "You don't have to insult me," she says. "I know you never liked me. I know you're jealous of me."

"Jealous of you?"

"Don't even try to deny it. And not only are you a weird freak, you're a liar, too. Weren't you at

Hank Hobbs's house with Detective Fusilli? Andy saw you go by the other day."

"But what does that have to do with —"

Marigold's eyes glitter with tears. "Just leave us alone," she says. "Leave all of us alone. Go back where you came from, I don't care. Just get lost."

Crying, she stumbles away. With last looks of death at me, her girlfriends follow.

Now I realize that the hallway is silent. No one is slamming a locker door. No one is chanting a rap song. No one is hooting with laughter at something someone else said.

They are all looking at me.

One of them is Andy Hassam. He stares at me from his open locker. The stare is anything but friendly.

It is instantly clear to me that my less-than-stellar social standing at Beewick High has now bottomed out. I am less than zero. I am finished.

And it's only ten after nine.

SIXTEEN

I get through the day. I don't know how. But time passes, and you have to go to class, and take your French quiz, and hide in the bathroom next to the gym during lunch period, and scurry to your classes while kids whisper about you, and then, boom, after about twelve thousand hours of agony, school is over and you can go home.

There are cliques in my high school, like all high schools, but it's small, so everyone sort of hangs together in a crisis, and Mason was having a crisis, and if Marigold's blaming me for it, well, kids just kind of go along with that. Nobody's mean to me or trips me on purpose or writes *SKANKY FREAK* on my locker, but nobody gives me a "hang in there" sign, either.

That feeling I had at my locker, that feeling of being completely alone in the world — it's still there. It's like I'm standing still, and Diego and Shay are moving away. What I thought was family is just three people living in a house.

I make my way home on my bike. The cool wind hits my face and feels good. I wish it were colder. I wish it were freezing. I wish that every time I start to cry, the wind would freeze my tears and they would break like glass.

Shay isn't home from work yet, and neither is Diego, so I'm on my own. It's only four o'clock, and it's close to dark. I turn on some lights and I still feel spooked. Even though I don't want to see them right now, I wish they were here.

"This is ridiculous," I say out loud.

What is it about this house that is spooking me?

And do I really want to know?

What I need is some hot-water therapy, I decide. I turn on the shower and wait for the water to get hot, then climb in. I let the water pound my back, sluice down my short hair. I scrub with Shay's special oatmeal soap, the kind that has little nubby pieces of oatmeal in it, the soap Diego swears has twigs in it, it hurts so much. I like how it feels, like I'm washing the whole day off my skin. I scrub until my skin is pink, and then I turn off the water and pull back the shower curtain and the light dims and there is blood on the curtain.

There is blood on the curtain and the curtain is on the floor and the body is lying on it.

When I wrap the curtain around the body, it makes a crackling plastic noise that makes me jump.

At least it covers his face.

It's a body. It's not a person. Not anymore. Don't think of it as a person. That's how you'll get through this.

It is so heavy to drag. But it's not far to the door. The smell is so awful.

I don't want to see this, I don't want to know this, I don't want to feel this. . . .

And I am myself again, my eyes wide open, standing in the bathtub. My hand is clutching the curtain.

I am shaking with cold, shaking with terror. I reach for the towel.

And then I hear it.

Footsteps.

Now, I know the footsteps in this house. Shay's quick step. Diego's work boots.

These are stranger's footsteps. I am not having a vision. I am hearing them.

I look over at the door. I can't seem to swallow, can't seem to move.

The doors in the house were shaved on the bottoms years ago, before Shay had the house, to make way for the horrible shag carpeting that Shay tore up. There's a good two or three inches of space at the bottom of the door.

So when someone moves, I see the shadow.

SEVENTEEN

I look around the bathroom for some kind of weapon. There isn't much damage you can inflict with a loofah.

I hear the footsteps, so soft outside the door. I hear them stop. I see the shadow. I know if I kneel down and look underneath the door, I could probably see shoes, but I'm too scared to move.

And what if I bend down to look, and someone is bending down at the other side of the door, looking at me?

That thought sends such terror through me that it makes me move. I lunge toward my pants hanging on the hook on the back of the door. My cell phone is in the pocket.

I punch out Joe's number. Why didn't I ever put him on speed dial?

Because I never thought I'd need him so fast.

I get his voice mail, but I pretend he picks up. If I can hear the person's footsteps, the person can hear me.

"Joe! Joe! There's someone in the house. I hear them. Come right away! You're already on your way over? Oh, hurry. Don't use the siren, maybe you can catch them. . . ."

I hear the footsteps retreating. Fast.

That's when my knees give way, and I fall on the floor. I feel myself shaking and I can't stop.

I can't get up. The floor is so cold.

The phone rings next to my hand. "Gracie! Gracie!"

It's Joe. He must have picked up on his voice mail.

"Joe, someone is here. Please, hurry."

"I'm on my way. I'm close. Is the intruder still there?"

"I . . . I don't know —"

It is as long as forever, but I hear footsteps in the house, and I know it's Joe. I realize I'm lying on the floor in a towel, and I struggle to my feet and get into my clothes as fast as I can.

Joe knocks on the door. "Gracie, open it. It's me. No one's here."

I open the door. My knees are shaking, and I fall into his arms while he fires questions at me, and I'm trying to talk, and he's gently sitting me down on the hall floor.

"This is where he died, Joe," I tell him. "This is where Billy was killed."

He frowns, not wanting to believe me. "Are you sure someone was here? There's no sign that some-one broke in —"

"I didn't lock the door. I never lock the door. I didn't imagine it, Joe!"

"No, I don't think you did."

Joe is looking past my shoulder. It is clear in the light from the living room lamp. A muddy footprint outside the bathroom door.

EIGHTEEN

It doesn't take the police long to figure out the brand of the shoe, an athletic shoe in a size that pretty much rules out the intruder being a woman. Within half a day, they discover that a pair was sold to Mason Patterson at the Athletic Aerie over in Ardsley. Then the police search the school, and the shoes are found dumped in the waste can in the gym. Way to go, Beewick Police Department.

There's only one problem — Mason has an alibi. He was hanging with two of his buddies, Andy and Dylan, goofing off in the woods outside school.

Or so they say.

I ask Joe what he thinks Mason's motive was, and for once he lets me in on what he's thinking. He's come over to give us the news, and he and Shay have a truly awkward conversation, and I offer to walk him to his car. We stand by his car in the driveway. Joe must be distracted, because he doesn't seem to mind answering my questions.

"He might have broken into your house just to scare you because he's got it in his head that you're a pipeline to me," Joe says. "The Pattersons are furious that I'm including their son in the investigation.

So just because he broke in doesn't mean he killed Hank Hobbs."

"Why *would* he kill Hank Hobbs?"

"Maybe Hobbs caught them at the house, they were in the middle of some prank, and he tried to stop them, and things went bad." Joe's hands are in his pockets, and he stares back at the house. Behind the lighted windows, Shay is moving around, preparing for evening, switching on lamps, bringing a wool throw to the sofa. She was wearing her work clothes, but she disappears and comes back in sweats. The woman can't bear to wear a piece of clothing with a zipper, I swear.

"Maybe Hobbs had his boat at the dock, and Mason was aboard, and pushed him or something, and he fell off into the water," I say. "So they take the boat out to sea and just hope the body never turns up."

"Not quite, Gracie," Joe says. "Leave the detecting to me, remember?"

Joe turns and opens his car door. He looks back at me. "Go back inside. I'll wait."

"You're going to wait for me to go back inside? It's right across the lawn!"

But the shadows are lengthening, and I suddenly do feel spooked. Joe just looks at me. So I turn obediently and start back across the lawn, secretly glad he is there to watch me.

★ ★ ★

I'm just waking up the next morning when I hear it. *Dah doh din daa do.* In my head, it's a familiar tune. But then I'm fully awake, and I realize it's not a tune, not really. It's a series of notes. Like something out of that movie *Close Encounters of the Third Kind*, when they communicate with the alien spaceship through this giant synthesizer.

Dah doh din daa do.

The tune is still in my head as I stumble into the kitchen for my morning cereal. Diego is chomping on some toast. We haven't really talked since the Marigold incident, or since Joe told us the footprint belonged to Mason's shoe.

"How're you doing?" he asks.

"Okay."

"Mom says I should take you to school today. She'll pick you up."

I look up, surprised. "Why?"

"Because she's worried about you, spook doozy."

Diego calls me spook doozy sometimes, and I don't mind. It's kind of cool to have a nickname, and he says it with affection. But this morning, it hits me wrong.

"I don't want to interfere with your morning plans," I say huffily.

"I talked to Marigold," Diego says. "She's sorry about what happened. She was upset. Her parents are freaking out."

"You told her that my father could be the

killer," I say, looking down into my cereal bowl. "You told her all about him."

I sneak a look at Diego. He doesn't look guilty, and that makes me more angry at him.

"But your father *could* be the murderer," he says. "You think that, too. And why shouldn't I tell Marigold that your father came to see you? She's my girlfriend."

"She told the whole *school* that he could be a murderer!"

"The whole school thinks that *Mason* could be a murderer. Looks like you're even."

He's not on my side. He's on Marigold's side.

What is family? It's people there to catch you when you fall. What happens when they step back, when they're looking at someone else so hard, they don't notice that you're falling?

Dah doh din daa do.

The music in my head sends a shudder through me. I am afraid of this house.

Diego gets up. "Let me know when you're ready to leave," he says.

Dah doh din daa do.

I realize something, something I picked up in my vision, and I didn't even register it.

The killer is thinking about killing someone again.

He is thinking about killing me.

NINETEEN

It is a cold Saturday morning before Thanksgiving. Nate and Shay meet at the lawyer's office so that Nate can sign over the house to Shay for me. I watch them sign about a million papers, and the whole time I'm thinking, *After this he'll leave.*

I'll never know him.

I'll never know what he really is.

They finish signing the papers. They shake hands.

"Can I talk to Gracie?" Nate asks Shay.

He has to ask permission. My own father has to ask permission to talk to me. This is one seriously screwed-up situation.

"Of course," Shay says.

We go outside. Shay's lawyer, Debra Peterson, has an office in her house, an old white frame farmhouse. We go out into the backyard. Nate climbs up on the picnic table and puts his feet on the bench. He motions for me to join him.

We look out at Debra's son's wooden swing set. Nate doesn't say anything for a moment. We just listen to the wind.

"How's this for an insane proposition?" he says. "You, me, and a turkey."

"What?"

"Why don't you come with me today for Thanksgiving vacation? You'd have to miss three days of school."

I shrug. Missing school is not exactly a hardship.

"I could drive you back on Sunday. Rachel would love to meet you. I'm under this delusion that we'd get along, all of us."

I'm so surprised, I don't know what to say.

"I'd really like you to come," he says in a very gentle voice.

I breathe in and breathe out. I stare at Deborah's son's playground set. I babysit for him sometimes. Jared.

There's a red ball on the grass. There's a green pail. A blue train car left underneath the swing. Here is a kid who is loved. You can just see it. You can see it in the living room, in the basket of toys. In the kitchen, stocked with granola bars and fruit and oatmeal cookies. You can see it in the framed photograph on Deborah's desk, of her son and her husband on the beach.

I can open my heart and feel how much he's loved.

I was loved. My mom loved me. But there was

always a shadow there, a shadow where a father should be.

I don't know if I can love my own father. But I do want to know him. I *need* to know him.

Nate peeks at me, but he bursts out laughing when he sees my face.

"Oh, man," he says. "It's not root canal. It's a nice house in the 'burbs." He nudges me with his shoulder. "Who knows, maybe you'll even like it."

And I think — *Where is home?* Beewick Island started to feel like home. Shay's house started to feel like home.

But people like Mason don't want me to feel at home here. And Shay and Diego are a unit, woven as strong as steel mesh. Shay has invited all my confidences, but kept so much of herself secret from me. Maybe the oppression I feel in that house now has more to do with how I feel about the people in it.

My father is a stranger. I don't know what sports he likes, or music. I don't know if he's grumpy in the morning. I don't know if he likes Christmas, or knows how to cook. I don't know any of the million details you're supposed to know about your father.

But something vibrates between us. We can pick up on a rhythm together. We can be silent together. We can hook on to a feeling and ride it, even if it's sadness.

It's something to go on. And it's somewhere to get to.

TWENTY

Shay sits with her mouth open for at least five seconds.

Then she shakes her head. "I can't let you."

"It's just Thanksgiving."

"But . . . we don't really know him, Gracie. We don't know anything about him, what he's been doing."

"He's been working. He got married."

"We only know what he's told us. And there was a murder here."

"If Joe thought he was a suspect, he wouldn't let him leave."

Shay shakes her head again. "I can't let you go."

"He's my father. I have a right to make this decision."

"I'm your guardian and I love you. I have a right to forbid you."

We stare at each other.

"I just want to know him, Shay," I say.

"I need to talk to him first," she says.

Shay talks to Nate. Shay calls Rachel. They talk for a long time. When she gets off, Shay finds me in my bedroom, where I'm lying down reading a book. "She sounds nice," she says. "I already called Nate and told him to pick you up. Go ahead and pack."

I've already packed. I point to my suitcase. She gives me this sad little grin.

"And wear your gloves," she says.

Nate pulls up and honks. I go outside. First Diego gives me a quick hug, and then Shay gathers me up into one of her enfolding extravaganzas.

"Just come back to us," she whispers in my ear.

I feel surprisingly throat-lumpy about this, as if Shay's fear is right, as if I'm leaving forever.

We don't say much as we drive to the ferry. Nate pulls in back of the line. I look a few cars ahead to see who else is in line. I realize that it's a Beewick Islander thing to do. You usually know at least one person in the ferry line if you've lived here long enough.

And sure enough, I see Zed's Subaru up ahead. We still have a few minutes left before the ferry, so I tell Nate I'll be right back.

Zed is reading a book behind the wheel when I approach. I have to tap on his window to get his attention. He looks up at me and I get the gift of his smile, which just about knocks me backward. For a moody, complicated individual, Zed can sell the simple stuff.

He gets out, even though it's started to rain. It's a Pacific Northwest rain, a mist that nobody would dream of carrying an umbrella for.

"Hey, heading to the city?" Zed asks.

I tilt my head toward Nate's car. "I'm going away for Thanksgiving. With my father."

"Oh, cool. You're coming back, though, right?"

Why is everyone asking me that? "I guess," I say.

"You guess?"

"Well. Things haven't been going so well here," I say. "Ever since Hank Hobbs got murdered, things are so screwy. School is completely wrong."

"I heard what happened," Zed says. "Marigold went ballistic on you. She and Mason are tight."

"Everybody keeps saying that, as though that's an excuse," I say angrily. "You islanders really hang together."

"Not really," Zed says mildly.

"I'm just so tired of not belonging anywhere," I say in a sudden rush. "I mean, I really feel tired, you know? Tired of making an effort all the time. School. Home." I wave around at the trees. "Here. And with Shay and Diego. Everyone of us tries so hard, and should we have to? Should a family have to try so hard?" Suddenly, the lump in my throat is back. I don't know why I've chosen this day to finally talk to Zed, and when I do, I blurt out my feelings like an idiot.

Zed's silver-moon eyes regard me carefully. I

wonder what he's thinking. I can't read him. Once, when I first met him, I read his sadness. His mother is dead, just like mine, and that's something you don't get over. His dad is an okay guy, but he works all the time, so Zed was basically raised by his dad's succession of live-in girlfriends. No wonder Zed seems remote. Here's a guy who's used to being left.

"What's a family?" Zed asks with a shrug. "A couple of people who lurch from crisis to crisis together. Maybe you just have to hang, Gracie. I don't know your dad. I just know Shay and Diego. If they were dealt to me as a new family, I'd be all over it. If I had to work it like work, I would."

The cars have left the ferry that just came in, and I hear the car engines start in the line. We're ready to board.

"Well, good-bye," I say.

"Have a good Thanksgiving," Zed says. "I'll see you when you get back."

I start back toward Nate's car. Everything seems to shimmer, the mist, the trees, the clouds, the sky. I feel as though I'm walking in a dream. A dream I've had forever. I'm walking toward my father, and he waits for me.

TWENTY-ONE

Nate lives in a town called Wallanan. It's one of those anywhere towns, neighborhoods made up of strip malls and developments, but it's plopped down in a beautiful area in the shadow of Mt. Rainier. If Rainier ever blows, the town will probably get swept all the way to Seattle.

I'm surprised as the streets we drive down become progressively more posh. The houses get bigger, the streets wider, the landscaping more lush. Finally, Nate pulls into the driveway of a huge pile of wood and glass. Three stories of fine living.

"Wow," I say. "What do you know. You're loaded. If I'd known, I would have made up with you sooner."

"Ha. We're not really loaded — Rachel just has a nose for real estate."

We haven't really talked much on the way down. We'd been content to let the silences ease us into each other's space. Now he smiles at me.

"I'm glad you came."

I see movement at the front window, and a moment later the front door opens and a woman comes running as we get out of the car. She grabs me and hugs me, something I wasn't expecting, and then steps back.

"Let me look at you," she says, so I feel I have permission to check her out, too.

For some reason I feel surprise, as if I'd been expecting to recognize her, even though Nate has never shown me a photograph of her. She's not really pretty, but she has thick dark-blond hair and nice hazel eyes. Her face is very long and thin, as though it's been stretched out an extra couple of inches. She's one of those women who give the illusion of being pretty until you look harder and start judging the length of a nose or the thinness of an upper lip. Attractive, I guess you'd say. She's dressed in jeans and a white sweater, and a pair of battered leather boots. When she hugs and kisses Nate, I get a good feeling from her. She really loves him. She wants this to work, all of it.

She wants a family.

"Come on, come in, you must be famished," Rachel says, which is something people always say to people after car trips.

The house is full of overstuffed furniture. Sofas and armchairs and window seats and love seats. Everywhere you look, there's a place to sink into. There are pillows and wool throws and footstools, magazines and books and flowers. I want to make fun of it, but I can't. So much effort went into it, so much time picking rugs and fabrics.

"I love decorating," Rachel says. "I had this catering business, and I sold it, and, boy, did I have time on my hands. Suddenly, I had time to shop. I used to have, like, a futon and a bookshelf and my cooking knives. That was it." She crosses her arms and squints at the house, as if she's seeing it through my eyes. "Sometimes I think I went a little overboard."

"No way," I say.

Rachel has made ham sandwiches and cheese sandwiches — "in case you're a vegetarian" — and an avocado sandwich — "in case you're a vegan." She has bottled iced tea and soda and water and milk. The refrigerator is crammed with food, and she has four kinds of cookies for dessert. I begin to sense that overboard might be a way of life for her.

Nate tells her about Beewick, and she listens, but she's noticing me the whole time, refilling my glass, getting up to fetch another napkin, pushing the plate of sandwiches over when I finish what I have. She gives me little smiles of encouragement, too.

I have never seen somebody so glad to see me in my life.

It doesn't take a psychic to figure her out. I am the cement to hold her and my father together. That, and the baby she wants so much.

"How about a tour?" Rachel asks when I'm done.

Nate heads off to do some business in the study, and Rachel and I wind through the house, through the pretty dining room with yellow walls, through the master bedroom suite, through the little "sewing room" that she uses for her office. "I gave Nate the office downstairs," she says. "He's going to handle the business end of things for our new venture."

"New venture?"

"We'll show it to you tomorrow." She waves her hand at her office. "I've mostly used this for my scrapbooking. I do stuff for me, and for friends. This will be the baby's room soon. We'd want her on the same floor for a while. I think it's bad luck to decorate ahead of time, but I have so many ideas. I think I'm going to paint clouds on the ceiling."

"That sounds pretty," I say.

"Come on, let me show you your room."

The guest room is about five times the size of my room at Shay's, with big windows that flood the room with the gray light of the afternoon. It has its own bathroom with a huge tub. Rachel has laid out lots of bath oils and bubble baths. There is a stack of thick blue towels resting on a little stool.

"I'll let you get settled," she says. "Then I can give a tour of the town, if you like."

I take a shower in a stall as big as a room. There's plenty of hot water, and the pipes don't knock. I don't have to worry about anybody else needing to use the bathroom. I get out and use two big towels to dry myself.

I get dressed again and start downstairs. I stop on the stairs when I hear Rachel and Nate talking in the living room.

"You just have to be patient, sweetheart," Nate says. "Something could come through any day now."

"It's just so hard, waiting . . ."

"Let's focus on the new business. There's a lot to do."

I enter the room, and they look up. Rachel looks teary, and I start to back out again, suddenly feeling like an intruder.

"No, it's okay, honey," Rachel says. She wipes at her cheeks and gives me a big smile. "We were just talking about the adoption."

"Adoption?" I knew they wanted to start a family, but I'd assumed that Rachel was trying to get pregnant.

"We're adopting a baby," Rachel says. "From Russia. Some days are just hard, that's all. You get your hopes up, and it turns out you have to keep waiting."

"Oh," I say. So I'll have a half-Spanish cousin and a Russian brother or sister. The thought fills me up, makes me smile. It sounds like a pretty cool family. "I'm sure everything will turn out okay," I say.

"Thank you, honey." Rachel springs up. "How

about a tour of the town? We can stop for ice cream or Starbucks or something."

"Sounds great," I say.

Nate says he'll stay home, and Rachel and I take off. She's a good driver, zipping around the streets in her little sports car.

"I had a business in Seattle, and I sold it to my partner," she says. "A big catering firm. I moved to Seattle from Ohio, and I didn't know a soul. Then all I did was work. I needed a break. So I took the money and put it into my house, and I have enough to live on for a bit until I figure out my next direction. I feel so lucky. I met Nate at the right time, and he's been so incredibly supportive of the adoption. What do you think of the name Sonia?"

"I like it."

"I want something that will connect her to her heritage. We asked for a girl."

She shows me the high school, the library, the places where the kids hang. Everything looks bigger than it does on Beewick. Bigger and newer. Everything is landscaped and lovely. I've landed in Pleasant Town.

"Who knows?" she says. "Maybe you'll want to stay." She reaches over and gently pats my hand for a second. "I want you to know that you're welcome, Gracie. Nate and I talked about it. We'd love to have you live with us. Summers, holidays, or all the time, if that's what you want. I mean, I wouldn't want to take you away from your aunt Shay. I'm just saying that we're here for you. I know your father wasn't there for you. But now he is." She takes her eyes off the road so she can look directly at me. "I promise you that."

But can one person promise another person that? I want to believe Rachel. I want to believe in her comfortable house, her vision of a family, her towels. It's all there for me to sink into. And I almost believe I can. Because somehow I know that she believes every word she says to me is true.

Yet there's some notes in my head that won't go away. Even as I talk to Rachel, even as I drive through a life that could be mine, I hear it:

Dah doh din daa do . . .

But what it's really saying is: *Be careful.*

TWENTY-TWO

The next day, Rachel and Nate take me to the building they're going to rent for their new business.

"Nate had the idea," Rachel tells me as she pulls into the parking lot of an upscale strip mall. "A café with a play-care area. There are tons of young kids in Wallanan. Lots of moms and dads. Nate thought, with my experience in food and his in business, we could really have something. We'd start out with only breakfast and lunch and coffee and snacks, and then we could eventually phase it into a kid-friendly dinner place. I was even thinking of calling it Kid Friendly, but Nate wants to call it Rachel's."

"I think it sounds more personal," Nate says. "Plus, the place is going to have Rachel's heart. It might as well have her name."

Rachel laces her fingers through his. "We just signed a lease on the space," she tells me. "See, there's a great kids clothing store here, and a day spa. Places moms come all the time. We need to do some renovation work on it. We want to open by February." She squeezes Nate's hand in her excitement. "Nate will handle most of the business end. And I'll be testing recipes for the next couple of months and over Christmas. It would be a fun time to be a houseguest, hint hint!"

We get out of the car. Rachel gets the keys out and opens the door. I guess I don't have much imagination, because all I see is a big empty space.

Rachel taps a heel on the floor. "We're putting in a new floor; this carpet has to go. And our idea is to have a little raised platform over here — kids love that — with chutes they can climb up and down on. You can sit here and have your coffee, or your salad, and watch your kid play. . . . And here is the kitchen, and we're going to redo the bathrooms. We've got the best contractor in town. You have to give him a hefty deposit, but we've nailed him for December. . . ." Rachel spins around. "You could be a waitress, Gracie! And go to school here, and live with us. . . ."

And I can see it. I can see going to that gleaming school, and biking over here and tying an apron over my jeans, and bringing nice moms like Rachel their chicken salads and their balsamic vinaigrettes. I can see living in that third-floor bedroom, getting to know my dad, starting all over in a new place, with the person who should have been at my side from the beginning.

Nate smiles at Rachel and turns to me. "No

pressure, Gracie. Of course we want you here, but we know you have a life on Beewick."

"Of course," Rachel says. "I just want her to know that she's welcome."

Nate slings an arm around my shoulders. "I hope she knows that already."

I feel his arm on my shoulders, and for once, I don't flinch. I like feeling the weight of it.

We head for the door, but a balding middle-aged man is coming in, a ring of keys dangling from his fist. "Rachel, Nate, how are you?"

"Howard, it's nice to see you," Rachel says. "We were just doing some planning of the space."

"Good, good. Listen, I just thought I'd speak to you, because I didn't get your check. I'm sure it's an oversight, but . . ."

"But we mailed it last week," Rachel says, frowning.

"Uh, no, we didn't, honey," Nate says. "Totally my fault, Howard. I had it in my pocket and I forgot to do it. I found it this morning and dropped it off at your office. I left it with your secretary. It should be there."

"Okay, I'm sure Monique forgot to tell me. Enjoy your day, folks."

Rachel and Nate start out, and we wait while she locks the door.

He lied.

I know it. I can feel it. I can feel the lie.

Things tumble in my brain, things I don't want to face.

You don't know him. Don't make him into something that you want him to be.

Something here isn't right. And I have to find out what it is.

TWENTY-THREE

The next morning, I watch from upstairs as a delivery truck from an office supply store drops off several bags at the front door. Nate signs for them. Rachel is out at the gym. I don't want to see Nate this morning, so I'm pretending to sleep late.

He glances up at my window, and I jump back.

One lie isn't much to go on, I tell myself. And I don't know for sure it's a lie.

But doubt has a way of spreading, until all you're doing is watching someone and wondering . . . *What else about you isn't true?*

If Nate lied about dropping off the check, he was just buying time. But for what? Had he spent the money already? The questions pound in my brain, until I can't think.

So I decide to start with what I know is true.

He grew up in Bristol, Rhode Island.

He was able to buy the house on Beewick because of an inheritance from his aunt.

He got through law school, but hated practicing law. He quit when he left D.C.

He worked as a realtor in New Mexico.

He lived in San Diego for a while and ran a surf shop.

He wrote a newspaper column somewhere in Pennsylvania.

He met Rachel in Seattle, where he worked in commercial real estate.

He loved my mother.

He loved me.

How much is true?

I decide to leave out feelings. I'll start with the simple stuff.

Nate is just leaving when I come downstairs. He kisses me on the top of my head. "Got to get up earlier if you want to catch the worms. Or something like that."

"Who wants to eat worms?" I say.

Rachel comes in the door, still dressed in her gym clothes. She stops when she sees the bags of office supplies. "You went to the store for me! Thank you!"

He leans over and kisses her. "Don't mention it. You do enough."

It's a small lie. Taking credit for something he didn't do. *Not such a big deal*, I tell myself as I grab a bagel and some juice.

Or is it? Do you tell one lie, and that makes it easier to tell the next one, and the next?

Nate leaves, and Rachel plops down in a kitchen chair and begins to leaf through a catalog of chairs. Every so often, she sticks a little Post-it flag on a page.

"We've got to order the chairs soon," she tells me. "They've got to be comfortable, but not too comfortable. You don't want people to stay forever. You need turnover. What do you think of these?"

She flips the catalog over so I can see. "Nice."

She puts a little Post-it strip on the page, but she suddenly looks up at me. "I hope you're not bored. Let me narrow down some choices here, and we can go shopping or something. Your dad won't be back until dinner."

"Sounds good," I say. "He's been out a lot since I've been here."

"Oh, honey, are you disappointed? It's just that things are coming together for the business, and there's a million details."

"No, it's fine, it's just that . . . I think of these questions I want to ask, because I don't really know that much about him, and then by the time I see him, I forget what they are."

Rachel closes the catalog. "Well, try me. When we first met, all we did was talk and talk. I know everything about him." She grins. "Well, almost everything. I asked him not to tell me about old girlfriends. I'm the jealous type. As a matter of fact,

I'm planning a surprise for him for Christmas — a scrapbook. I've got plenty of photos and mementos from our time together, of course, but whew, I never met anyone who could stick all his photographs into one envelope. It's like the man doesn't have a past." Rachel's hand flies to her mouth. "Oh, honey, I didn't mean . . . I mean, of course he does, of course he has a past. Most of the photographs he saved were of you. I just mean, he moved around a lot, and . . ."

"It's okay," I say. "I know you didn't mean it." I want to keep her talking about Nate. "I know he grew up in Rhode Island, but I don't know much about my grandparents. I never met them, and neither did my mother. They died before she met my father."

"William and Eleanor," Rachel says, nodding. "William died of cancer quite young."

Ding. He died of cancer? Nate told me that he killed himself.

"Nate's mom died of a heart attack when he was in high school. So tragic." She leans forward and puts her hands on my hands. "So you see, you have so much in common. He doesn't like to talk about it, and I know you don't, either. But there are so many things you can share."

But I'm not interested in sharing grief. "What about his aunt, the one that left him money?"

"Jane," Rachel says. "She left him a bundle, I guess. He was able to buy that house on Beewick — which I'm so glad will be yours one day — and pay for law school, too."

Ding. I'd always heard from my mom that she put my dad through law school.

Two lies in about three seconds.

But they aren't just lies. They're someplace to start. Someplace to begin to figure out who Nathaniel Millard really is.

I tell Rachel and Nate that I made a date to see a friend in Seattle on Wednesday, so they drop me at the bus. I've already called Ryan, who told me he was "awesomely available" to help.

I meet him at his "office," a cyber café somewhere on the outskirts of Belltown, this very cool neighborhood in Seattle. I recognize his red hair and geek glasses as soon as I walk in. He's sitting at a back table with a supersize soda and a table littered with *People* and *US Weekly* magazines. He pushes them aside to make room for me.

"Celebrity worship is my life," he says. "Have a seat. Can I get you a soda or coffee or something? My treat, as long as it's under three dollars."

I stand back up. "I'll get it. And I'll bring back some food, too. Cookies or muffins?"

"Cookies, for sure."

I order a cup of tea and pick up two fudge cookies as big as salad plates.

"Awesome!" he says approvingly as he accepts the cookie. "I work better with a massive sugar rush." He flips open his laptop and cracks his knuckles. "Now, let us begin to reveal the real Nate Millard. Tell me what you need, and I'll open the portals of cybertown."

I take a bite of cookie and push over a piece of paper. I've written the names of Nate's parents, his aunt, and his full name. "Everything there is to know about them."

Ryan's fingers fly over the keyboard. He's an astute Googler, but he also belongs to this subscription newsnet site that allows him to search more efficiently and faster than I can.

He finds Eleanor Millard's death notice in the Providence paper, and the funeral notice about my grandfather. So far Nate's stories check out, at least about when they died. But Ryan frowns as he searches for Jane Millard.

"Millard bequest," he murmurs. "Wait, let me go back a few years. . . ."

"What?"

"Here we go. Jane Grace Millard. She was on the board of the local animal shelter."

"Grace?" Had I been named after my father's aunt? I never knew that.

"Yeah, wait . . . it's a family name. There are Graces and Millards all over the place in that part of Rhode Island. Looks like you might have a couple hundred second and third cousins once removed. Here we go — Jane Grace Millard died June second, 1988."

"What? That doesn't make sense." I quickly do the math. That means she died *after* Shay had bought the house.

"Newspapers don't lie. Well, scratch that — they lie all the time, I guess, but not about death notices. Yeah, and look, her whole estate went to the animal hospital."

So there was no inheritance.

So where did Nate get the money?

He put himself through school. He said. His father left him nothing. He said. The only money he ever had came from his Aunt Jane, who was the only one, he said, who really loved him.

"All right, let's get cracking on Nathaniel," Ryan says. "Not much coming up here. Nothing, in fact."

I watch Ryan chew his cookie and type and mouse-click. "Whoa. Whoa, whoa, whoa."

"What?"

I can see by his face that he doesn't want to show me. But he pushes the laptop over so I can see.

It's a Web site called *DEADBEAT DADS*. Women who have been abandoned post their husbands' names and photos on the site. And there he is, Nate, smiling, by a backyard grill.

"Tampa, Florida?" I ask. "Nathaniel Grace Millard, missing since 1998. Two kids?"

"Bunny and Ben," Ryan says. "Aw."

Ryan takes the laptop back as I sit, stunned.

Bunny. The pale blond girl with the stuffed rabbit. His daughter.

"Searching under the name Nate Grace now. Sometimes dudes on the run use variants on their names to . . . uh-oh."

I look over. It's a Web site created by Cheryl Anne Hinker from Factoryville, Pennsylvania.

HAVE YOU SEEN THIS MAN?

It's Nate.

He owes her money. He left town with it — and their wedding album.

"Whoa, serial sleazebag," Ryan says. He peers at me anxiously. "Some cold water or something? You look sort of green."

"Who is he?" I ask. "Who's my dad?"

"I'm going to have to break it to you gently, goddess Gracie," Ryan says. "He's a crook."

TWENTY-FOUR

A crook.

I've waited all my life to meet him. Even while I told myself I didn't need him, I did. Even while I told myself it didn't matter what he was or wasn't, it did.

Why had he come to Beewick Island? I no longer believed he had come there for me. Someone who lied his way through his life had to be lying now. Someone who always had an ulterior motive had to have one now.

I stare out at the highway and listen to the sound of the bus wheels whining on the wet road. It's raining, a true hard rain, not a Northwest mist. When I lean against my window, my breath fogs the glass. I keep wiping it with my hand. The window fogs and clears, fogs and clears. The road disappears and appears again. All the way back to him.

Nate is waiting in the car at the bus stop. I walk over to the car and get in.

"Have a good time with your friend?"

"Awesome," I say.

But he knows me now. He gives me a look, as if

he knows something is wrong. I look out the window and slump in my seat, teenage body language for "don't ask." He doesn't. He thinks I'm bummed because of a boy. Good.

"You should see what Rachel is cooking for tomorrow," he says, pulling out into traffic. "It'll just be the three of us, but she's making enough for a truck stop."

I suddenly feel enormously sorry for Rachel. She loves him. She does everything she can to please him. *Ask me. I know everything about him.* I remember her confidence, the love in her eyes. I'm so furious at him now, I could kick him out the car door into traffic.

"Rachel's great," I say. "You're lucky."

He gives me another sharp look, because he hears the acid in my tone. He coasts to a stop at a traffic light. He taps my knee. "Don't sweat it, kiddo. Teenage guys don't know anything."

"Oh," I say, "and when they're adults, they're so much smarter?"

"Ouch," he says. "Good point."

I watch his hands on the wheel, and I wonder if they could have murdered someone. Could he have hit Hank Hobbs and pushed him off a boat, then stood by and waited until he drowned?

The money.

I suddenly realize where he got the money for the down payment. I can't believe it's taken me so long to put it together.

Billy Applegate had gotten secret documents that would expose Monvor. But something happened. They disappeared. Billy believed that someone in the group had stolen them. Someone had sold them out for money.

How much money? Enough for half a down payment on a rundown house?

Why not?

But the question still hammers at me. If all this is true, I still don't know why Nate would come back to Beewick. If it wasn't for me, then why? Did he come back to kill Hank Hobbs?

That night, I set my alarm for three A.M. When it goes off, I almost catapult out of bed. My heart slams in my chest, and I have to force myself to calm down.

If I'm going to do this, I have to be careful. At this rate, my heart is hammering so loudly it will wake up the house.

I tiptoe to the stairs and pause on the second-floor landing. I listen carefully, but behind the door of the master bedroom, there is no sound, even of snoring. I keep going downstairs.

I have to move slowly in the unfamiliar house. It's so dark, and there's so much furniture. I shuffle my feet along, peering as the shadowy forms turn into end tables and ottomans in the huge living room.

I push open the door to the study. I'm going to

have to risk a light. If I get caught, I can say I couldn't sleep and I came down to surf the Web.

The desk is pretty neat. There are piles of folders on the top. I go through them quickly: the lease on the restaurant space, different kitchen catalogs, permit applications. There's one file marked ADOPTION. Another says MENU PLANS. Nothing I didn't know about. No secrets.

But secrets wouldn't be on top of the desk.

I start going through the drawers. I get out a big checkbook, a binder for the business checks. MILLARD/TOBIN ENTERPRISES. I leaf back through the record and see a check to the landlord made out for six thousand dollars. I flip back to see the running balance in the register. I pull out a bank statement and study that. I'm no accountant, so what do I know? It looks fine to me. But I'm sure Nate never delivered that check.

Then I see some numbers written in a small hand on the first page of the register. I'm guessing, but I bet the numbers are a password.

I boot up the computer. I go to the bank's Web site. There's a box for entering a password and one for a user name. Under PASSWORD, I type in the numbers I saw.

USER NAME. I try *RACHEL.* I can't get in. *NATE.* Still can't. *NATHANIEL.*

I try their full names. I try Rachel's maiden name. Nothing.

I hesitate, then type in *SONIA*.

I'm in.

I look at the bank balance, then back at the register. There's a twelve thousand dollar difference.

He's been writing the checks. He just hasn't been mailing them.

He was busted by the landlord. But I bet he's stalling him. I bet he gave him another story, and the landlord is giving him another day or so.

I feel sick, sick at heart. I know what he's planning now. He's going to leave her, and soon, before his lies are discovered. How could he be so heartless?

And then I think of Cheryl Ann in Pennsylvania.

The family in Tampa.

Me.

I go through the drawers, but there's nothing left to find. Rachel has left the business to Nate. She won't find out until he leaves, when she has to look up her own bank balance and discover the truth.

What I need to find out is more personal things. If only there were something I could get a reading off of. I usually run away from visions, but now I need one. I need to see the way to the truth.

As a matter of fact, I'm planning a surprise for him for Christmas — a scrapbook.

She has photographs. Old photographs.

If I search Rachel's office and get caught, what excuse could I give for being there?

I just can't get caught.

I switch off the lamp in the office and climb the stairs. I listen on the landing. Nothing.

I tiptoe into Rachel's office. I close the door, glad it doesn't squeak. I switch on the lamp on her worktable.

Rachel is very organized. There are photos, pieces of nice paper, calligraphic pens, glue sticks, paste-on lettering, different kinds of scissors, those little black corners people put on photographs. There are files labeled HOUSE and VACATIONS and BABY. I look in the baby file. She's already collecting things to put in the scrapbook — a line drawing of baby shoes. Samples of birth announcements. Pink labels.

I search through the files until I find it. NATE.

I open the accordion file. I thumb through the things that look current — photographs of Nate and Rachel, restaurant menus, ticket stubs. There is a separate envelope inside and I slip it out. It's full of old photographs.

The first one is of me.

I'm a baby. My mom is holding me in the hospital. A pink balloon rises above her head. Her blond hair is sticking up in a funny way, but who has a good hair day after giving birth? What you really notice is her smile. Her big, generous, goofy smile.

I swallow and blink. It just tears me, how grief never stops. It hits you when you're not looking, it spins your head around. It makes you gasp with the shock of it.

I put that photograph aside and keep looking.

There is a photograph of Nate as a boy standing in front of a brick house with a porch. He has dark hair and his hands are shoved into the pockets of his jeans. I am shocked to see how much he looks like me.

And then there are the photographs I'm hoping for. Beewick Island. I recognize it immediately. It's a shot of kids swimming at what the kids on Beewick call Fishstick Cove, since you can see the restaurants across the bay. It's a popular place to swim in the summertime because the water is fairly warm. I recognize Nate immediately, then Shay. She is dressed in cutoffs and a white T-shirt and is about fifteen pounds thinner. I touch her image, but I don't get an image from that smiling girl. And then I look at the young man by her side and get a chill, and I know that this is Billy Applegate.

He's got a cherubic face with round cheeks. Not what I expected. He's thin and wiry and good-looking. One of his hands rests on Shay's ankle.

A few days, or weeks, from when this picture is taken, he'll be murdered.

I don't even know him, and I feel sorrow for him. Because he died young. Because he didn't deserve to die.

I push the photograph to one side.

The next photograph is of Nate and Shay and my mother. It takes me a moment to recognize where it was taken. It's Shay's house. I recognize the windows of the back room, the mudroom that Diego and Shay turned into a bedroom for me. It's filled with trash, and two of the windowpanes are cracked. The three of them are holding up cans of soda in a toast and grinning for the camera.

The third photograph is taken from the hallway looking toward the bathroom. On the floor is an awful pinky-orangey shag carpet. Shay hadn't exaggerated the horror.

Shay and Nate are standing in the bathtub. Shay is holding her nose and making a comical face. Nate is waving a sponge. A mildewy shower curtain is pushed all the way to one side.

I recognize the curtain. Clear, with palm trees on it.

The body through the curtain.

The blood on the plastic.

Someone breathing, hard. Someone trying not to panic.

The last photograph is an old Polaroid, a snap-shot. It is of Nate and a man it takes me a long second to realize is Jeff Ferris. They are wearing kerchiefs tied around their heads, and they've painted on fake curly mustaches. They're at a party. People in costume swirl around them, dancing. The women are wearing long dresses, some with aprons, others with big petticoats. Some of them are wearing white wigs with long curls. Some of the men are wearing knickers and white stockings.

This must be the party Nate told me about. The local who had sneaked him in had been Jeff Ferris. That made sense. Jeff was his realtor.

We met at a Bastille Day party at the Beewick Club. . . .

I look at the other faces. I don't need to see him. I know Hank Hobbs was there.

Which means Nate could have met him.

Which means Nate could have lied.

Then I remember something else. The surf shop he owned in San Diego. Would someone who couldn't swim run a surf shop? You have to be a pretty good swimmer to surf.

I'm not much of a swimmer. He lied about that, too. Why would someone lie about that if they didn't have something to hide?

I hear footsteps outside in the hall. They are heavy. It's Nate.

I lunge for the lamp, almost knock it over. I turn

out the light and hold it before it crashes to the floor. Then I quickly stuff the photographs back into the envelope and shove it all back where I found it.

I run to the door and listen.

I hear a toilet flush. Footsteps start back toward the bedroom.

I run back to my room. I hug my knees and wait until first light. Until I can call Shay.

TWENTY-FIVE

"Gracie!" The relief and pleasure in Shay's voice sends warmth through me. "I was just sitting here with my coffee, thinking of you. I'm so glad you called."

I close my eyes and think of Shay's tiny dining room, the room that sticks out from the side of the house, that's big enough only for her long farm table and chairs. When we have people over for dinner, they have to crawl over each other to get to the bathroom. Shay's tiny house is so different from Rachel's. Shay doesn't have near the amount of sofas and pillows and room, but her house is always crammed full of guests and laughter and conversations. Rachel has a house that's filled with furniture but no people.

"Wait a minute, why are you calling? Is everything okay?"

"I just wanted to wish you Happy Thanksgiving."

"It's six-thirty in the morning. Tell me another one."

I flop over in bed and cradle the receiver. I keep

my voice low, even though I'm pretty sure Rachel and Nate are still sleeping.

"I guess I'm homesick."

She gives a laugh of pleasure. "Good. I mean, I hope you're having a good time with your father. But that makes me feel good."

"I was thinking about your house."

"*Our* house."

"Our house. I saw some pictures of it last night. When you first bought it. There was this really hideous carpet —"

"Hoo, I'll say. That color! Like a bruised cantaloupe."

"Nate is in the pictures. And my mom is in one of them. Do you remember who took them?"

"I don't remember. . . . I don't have copies of them. I think those were taken on closing day. We went over to celebrate. The house was a mess, but we felt like we'd just bought the Taj Mahal. Well, I did. But the work ahead of us was enormous. Nate started that night. He took out that carpet and the curtains and cleaned the floors, for a surprise for me and Carrie. It smelled a little better after that. But only a little. We threw open all the windows for weeks."

Nate took up the carpet and cleaned? He hasn't rinsed a dish since I've been here.

I'm scared, I want to tell Shay. *I want to come home.*

But I have one more thing to do here. So instead, I say "Happy Thanksgiving" again and hang up.

Look, I'm not good with holidays anyway. I've had two serious crashes on Christmas since mom died, and my birthday just makes me sad. But I didn't know how bad it could get until I was spending Thanksgiving with two strangers, one of whom could be my dad the murderer.

Rachel has gone all out. Butternut squash soup. Turkey, stuffing, creamed onions. Mashed potatoes and sweet potato casserole. Carrots. String beans. And two kinds of pie.

It's all good, but I can't eat. Every bite sticks in my throat. I have to pretend to eat, pretend to join in the conversation, but I can't stop thinking of what happened to Billy Applegate and Hank Hobbs.

And Rachel. Is she in danger, too?

In the middle of the pumpkin and the apple pies, the phone rings. Rachel gets up, a smile on her face. "That's probably my parents. I left a message before."

We hear her say hello in the kitchen.

Nate looks at me. "What's up, kiddo?"

"What?"

"You're not yourself."

"I'm in a food coma."

"You hardly touched your food."

"It's just weird, being here, I guess."

He puts his fork down. "You must miss her on holidays."

"I miss her every day."

"But it's worse on holidays, isn't it? It's like you're running on empty."

Yes, that's exactly what it's like.

"I always hated holidays myself," he says.

Suddenly, we hear Rachel sob.

We push our chairs back and hurry into the kitchen.

"Honey, what it is it?"

Rachel looks up him, tears streaming down her face, her hand still on the phone in its cradle. But she's smiling. "Our baby. Sonia. Our baby is ready for us. She's ready to come home."

Nate rushes to gather Rachel in his arms. "That's great, honey. That's great."

Does he mean it? If he doesn't, he's a great actor.

But isn't that the point? That he's a great actor? A con man?

Rachel swipes at her tears. "We have to leave for Moscow within a few days, they said. There's so much to do, I can't think. . . ."

"I'll take care of everything," Nate says. "Our passports are ready, you have baby clothes for Sonia, you even have diapers! Don't worry, sweetie, we're set. I'll buy the tickets."

Rachel holds out her hand to me. "Gracie. Gracie, I'm so sorry to cut your visit short. It's just that, they said we'd have very little notice —"

"I understand," I say. "It's okay. I can take the bus back."

"No," Nate says. "I'll drive you. I can do the trip in a day, then swing back here for the flight."

But he won't come back, I know. He'll take me back, but he'll keep going. He'll have her money, probably all the money she was going to use to pay for Sonia, the money for the tickets, everything. He'll clean out the business account. And he'll keep driving, maybe to Canada. I know it.

He'll leave her, just like he left all the others.

TWENTY-SIX

Rachel starts to call her family in Ohio to tell them the news. The kitchen is full of her voice, her laughter. Nate and I do the dishes. As he scrapes, I rinse and put things in the dishwasher, carefully choosing the right slots for the serving pieces, the pitchers, the gravy boat. He scrubs the pots while I wipe down the counters. He puts away the leftovers while I dry the crystal. We do all this half-listening to Rachel.

Yes, they just called me. . . .

I don't know, we haven't looked up flights yet, but maybe Saturday. . . .

Lots of paperwork and things, but we'll maybe be back in two weeks. . . .

I know, it will be cold, we have plenty of warm things for the baby. . . .

You will? Oh, you doll, you, thank you. . . .

Isn't it strange, I think, *that Nate has no one to call? He's about to be a father, after all.*

Every so often, he puts his hand on Rachel's shoulder as he goes by. There is so much trust in the way she covers his hand with her own. He leans over and kisses the top of her head.

My hands shake, and I can't see for a moment, as rage fills me up. These are things he did with mom. He touched her gently. He smiled at her. He listened to her plans. And all the time, he was waiting to leave us. Wanting to leave us.

Did he steal from mom, too? I don't know. It's not something she would have told me, I realize. She would rather me think of my dad as a flake than a crook.

After all the dishes are done and the leftovers put away, Nate sits at the kitchen table with Rachel to make plans. I go upstairs. On the way, I sneak back into Rachel's office. I slip out the photograph of Nate at the Bastille Day party. I tuck it in my pocket. I need something to show Joe, proof that Nate had known Hank Hobbs.

Turn my own dad in? You betcha.

Here is what I think happened twenty years ago.

Billy Applegate broke into Hank Hobbs's house and stole the incriminating memo. But somehow Nate got hold of it — stole it from Billy and gave it back to Hank Hobbs — for a price. That's how he got the money for the down payment. Maybe he never expected to go through with the house, but he did.

Billy suspected Nate and confronted him at the house. Nate killed him.

And then, years later, Nate bumps into Hank

Hobbs somewhere, probably in Seattle. Hobbs remembers him as the guy he'd bribed all those years ago. Maybe something happened, maybe something clicked, maybe Hank Hobbs suddenly realized that Nate had killed Billy. So Nate killed Hank Hobbs. Nate pushed him off the boat and watched him drown.

It all makes sense, but I feel like I'm missing something.

I toss and turn for a long time, but I finally fall asleep. I fall into a dream so deep, I can't wake up.

I dream that I'm breathing dirt. There's mud in my mouth and nose, and I can't get it out.

I'm being sucked down through the bed. Things are sliding against my skin, dragging against me. I feel oozy mud between my fingers, between my toes, in my mouth. I am drowning in a swamp.

Spiky branches are above me, and I try to grab them. Ferns crumble in my fingers.

It seems to take an enormous effort to wake myself up. I spring up from the bed and run to the bathroom. I switch on the light and splash my face with cold water. Over and over until I can breathe again.

When I come up, pushing my wet hair behind my ears, I suddenly know, with a blazing certainty, why Nate was on Beewick. It wasn't just to kill Hank Hobbs.

The wetlands reclamation project.

The land is being drained. On Saturday.

And the body of Billy Applegate will surface.

Did he hope the killing of Hank Hobbs would delay it? Stop that last-minute million-dollar grant? He was wrong.

Did he hope to find out more, to find out exactly when the draining would happen? Did Shay tell him? Is that why he's planning to leave Rachel, before the body is found and a murder investigation is reopened?

I need to get back. I need to find out. I need to know where Billy Applegate lies.

The next day, I wait in my room until he leaves on an errand. I pull on my jacket and make sure the photograph is still in my pocket. I can't let them know I'm leaving, because I'm afraid he'll track me down.

She's sitting at the kitchen table, a teapot next to her elbow and a mug of tea in one hand, while she writes a list with the other.

"Hey, sleepyhead," she says. "There's so much to remember, I'm making lists like crazy. Can I get you breakfast? Lunch?"

"I thought I'd go for a run."

"A run? But it's raining."

"It's always raining."

She laughs. "True. Seize the day, I guess — I'll

stick with hot tea. I'll have some breakfast for you when you get back."

I can't tell her. I can't tip him off. But I can't leave her like this, either.

"You've been really nice to me," I say. "I just wanted to tell you — I'm really glad about Sonia. She couldn't have a better mother."

Her eyes fill with tears. "That means a lot."

I go to the door and open it. "Just . . . be careful."

I shut the door on her puzzled frown. And then I start to run.

I catch the bus to Seattle. I have to wait another hour to catch the next bus, the one that will take me to the ferry. It's late. By the time I board, it's past two o'clock.

The bus lets me off at the ferry. I am so glad when my feet hit the deck. I stand at the railing, my back to the line of cars driving aboard. I face the island in the distance.

The ferry ride is so short that most people don't get out of their cars. Just the pedestrians, like me, and the bicyclists, and a few people wanting to stretch their legs before we dock.

I am lucky. I see Nate racing up the stairs before he sees me. I see him searching the deck, his head swiveling. I feel his urgency and his anger.

I duck down the left stairway, down to the deck

where the cars are. I keep my head low. He'll have to get back into his car in three minutes, when the ferry docks. I am so glad it's only a twelve-minute trip.

I don't see him again. I stay hidden. The ferry begins its docking maneuvers. Car engines start up. The slow exodus begins, people patiently lining up and driving off.

I see his Volvo bump off the ferry and zoom away.

I don't have much time.

TWENTY-SEVEN

It's almost dusk when I reach the swamp. I check the shadows and realize I don't have much daylight left. Just enough time to go in, see what I can pick up, and leave. If I can pinpoint the area where I think Billy Applegate's body lies, I'll have more leverage with Joe. It's a big area, and I want to be sure. I know the final drainage will take place early tomorrow, and I need more than hunches to get Joe out here.

The first place Nate will go will be Shay's. She'll probably freak, and he'll have to stay while she calls Rachel, calls Joe, calls everybody she can think of. I hate to put her through another disappearance of mine, but I can be home within the hour, or even sooner, if I'm lucky. I've made sure my cell phone is off, so I won't have to feel guilty about ignoring the calls for a while. I'm not ready to talk to anyone yet.

I know the wetlands area well, thanks to Shay. She actually enjoys hiking around in this stuff. The reclamation project has used narrow wood decking to build a trail through the swampy area to make it easier for the scientists to gather information over the past years. I know the way, since Shay has brought me out here many times. I used to think Shay's work was boring when I first got here. Well, I still think it's boring, but I sure have learned a lot about wetlands.

I hadn't counted on how the trees would block the remaining light in the sky. I wish I'd thought to bring a flashlight. I decide I'll only go another couple of hundred yards and then try to get a sense of what I'm looking for. I remember my vision — I remember the way the branches hung, and the ferns that lay like a blanket nearby.

The only trouble is, I don't know if the vision was of the present or the past. If it was the past, then things have changed since then — trees have died, have grown, ferns have given way to bushes and scrub.

But the landscape is looking familiar now, and I can feel the back of my neck prickle, and it isn't from the falling mist. I'm close. I know it.

There was once a pond here. The water has been draining for weeks. I put one foot out and sink, but not too deeply. I know if I walk through these trees, I will find a dry area to stand on. I know there will be ferns and dead leaves. I know because I saw it.

The ground sucks at my shoes, and I have to drag my feet out while I walk, a creepy sensation. Something is pulling me onward, and I could no more resist it than I could a cold drink on a hot day. It will bring me relief, somehow. I will *know*. I will know everything that happened. I will know my father. I will know what is broken and can never be fixed, and I will know how to go on.

The land is firm, just as I'd seen. It used to be underwater. The light is fading, but I can see something shine ahead. A glint.

I go closer. Mud-smeared, filthy, but still intact. The edge of a shower curtain.

And unmistakably, a human hand.

I want to run, but I can't, the mud is too thick. But the panic inside me is rising, and I can't seem to make headway. The trail is just yards away, but it might as well be a mile.

I fumble for my cell phone in the pocket of my jacket. I stab out Joe's number.

I hear the tones chime.

And I understand at last what I've been hearing in my head.

Dah doh din daa do . . .

It wasn't a tune. It was the electronic tones of numbers on a keypad.

I disconnect the call before it rings. Slowly, I punch out numbers, trying to match the tones. It takes me a while, but I get it at last. 7 1 4 8 6.

It's not a phone number. What is it? I play the tones once, twice. I close my eyes and feel the keypad, concentrating as I listen.

I see fingers stabbing a keypad.

I see Jefferson Ferris pushing the alarm code at his house.

Seven. One. Four. Eight. Six.

And behind my closed eyes, those numbers form a date. July 14, 1986.

July fourteenth. Bastille Day.

We met at a Bastille Day party.

The photograph of Nate at the party.

What am I missing? What is there that I can't see?

"These days we have to remember so many codes and passwords, it's a wonder our heads don't explode. My secret system is to code everything on my dog's birthday."

"You remember your dog's birthday?"

"No. That's the problem."

People pick codes that mean something to them. Wedding anniversaries. Their children's birth dates. Jeff Ferris's code was the same date that Hank Hobbs met Betsy Dunwoody. But why?

And then I remember something. When Hobbs's house was broken into twenty years ago, the alarm didn't go off. He'd told the police that he thought he'd set it. What if he had? What if the thief knew the code?

What if Hobbs used the date he had met his fiancée for his code? What if someone knew that?

Someone like Nate? He'd been at the dance.

He'd been at the dance with Jeff Ferris.

Dad sold Hobbs his first house on Beewick. A big sale for us, back then.

If Jeff Ferris knew Hank Hobbs's alarm code, he could have been the one to steal the file and pass it along to Billy. But why?

So many whys, and it all happened so long ago. I'm confused now. Confused by things I've seen, confused by what people say and what they don't say. Confused by facts that jumble together in my head. Confused by all my visions. Everything seemed to point in one direction, but now it feels as though they point in so many directions, sending me spinning like a top, bouncing from one thought to another.

Nate and Jeff at the Bastille Day dance.

I was never a great swimmer. . . .

Jeff Ferris is a great guy. He coaches at the high school. He knows Mason and Dylan, who are both on the swim team. . . .

I can't untangle this. All I can do is go straight to Joe and dump it on him.

I turn my back on the shower curtain, but suddenly, I see it again.

The shower curtain rips off the rod. It falls to the bathroom floor. He drags the body onto it. The carpet is soaked with blood. He rolls the shower curtain around the body. It is hard to do because his hands are shaking so badly. He rolls the body into the curtain. Beads of sweat roll down his nose and drop, drop, drop onto the curtain. He secures the curtain with twine. It is no longer Billy he sees. He just sees . . . a body. Soon he will forget this. He will move on. After he lays Billy to rest. Not Billy. The body. The body.

Hobbs treads water. Blood trickles into the water. He's getting tired. The boat circles him, chugging. Circling. Circling. Waiting . . .

I feel the fear of Hank Hobbs as the cold water locks him into a paralysis that is pure terror.

He doesn't have the strength to scream, or the breath. The scream is inside his head. It is inside my head, and it is so loud that at first I don't hear the sound of someone tramping through the marsh and dragging something behind him.

TWENTY-EIGHT

I look down as I drop the phone. It seems to fall in slow motion as I bend to catch it. It disappears into the murky water.

I sink into the muck as I drop to my knees to search. My hands are in the muddy water and I'm crying now, crying hard, as Jeff Ferris appears, dragging a sled. Something a kid would use on a snowy day, flat on the bottom, curled in front. A coil of rope is slung around his shoulder. He's carrying a shovel.

He looks surprised and dismayed to see me. "Is that you, Gracie? What are you doing here?"

"I'm here . . . looking," I say, stammering, "with Shay and Joe."

His eyes shift. "Where are they? I didn't see a car."

"No? Oh, they're around," I say. "Shay wanted to do a few things before tomorrow. . . . You know, the last draining will take place. . . ."

I can feel something shift. He narrows his eyes, and he smiles. "You're lying." He takes a step closer to me. "Why are you lying, Gracie?"

"I'm not," I say, taking a step back. I can't help it.

"You look afraid. If one were paranoid, one might think that you suspected me of something."

I search for something to say, but there is nothing to say. He knows I suspect him. He knows Shay and Joe aren't here.

"It's really a drag, having a psychic girl around," Jeff says, hitching the rope higher on his arm. "You gave me some sleepless nights, especially after I caught you at my house."

"I don't know what you mean —"

"Yeah, you do."

"It was you," I say. "You're the one who broke into Shay's house."

"I didn't break in. The door was open. Get your facts straight." Jeff's face turns nasty for a minute. "I wasn't going to hurt you. I just wanted to scare you off, that's all. And make you think it was Mason."

"The shoes . . ."

"I got them from Mason's locker — he always leaves it open. Beewick is such a friendly place. That's one of the reasons I like it."

"You wore his shoes. And then you threw them away at school so the police would find them."

"So you see, I didn't want to kill you." Jeff looks at me sadly. "And now it looks like I have to. I don't want to, mind you. But I just want you to know — I can. I turned this corner when I killed Billy. I didn't know it at the time. At the time, I just thought, oh boy, I'll never do *this* again. Have I learned *my* lesson. Hoo boy. But then, when I killed Hank Hobbs, it wasn't so hard. Gets easier all the time."

I'm so cold. I'm so very cold.

"Hate to do it to Shay. She's a nice lady. But you haven't been here very long. It's not like you're her kid or anything."

Is he crazy? He's saying these things in a totally normal tone of voice. Yet he means them. I know he's capable of killing me. I can see it in the odd, glassy way he's looking at me. His bland features are suddenly ugly. I wish I could go back to teasing him behind his back with Diego. I wish he'd ask me "How's the house?"

I wish I hadn't been so stupid.

I wish I wasn't here.

"And this is great, in a way, because you can help me move Billy's body."

"*What?*"

"I've got the place all picked out. Nobody will find it. Up on the north end of the island, where the tides will take him all the way to Canada. That was my mistake last time — I didn't know the island well enough. The whole thing will be real quick, I promise."

"You're crazy."

"No, I'm not. I just have a job to do."

I have to do what they do in the movies. Get him talking.

"Why did you do it?" I ask. "Why did you kill Billy?"

He looks annoyed. "Well, I didn't mean to. That's the whole point."

"What happened?"

It's getting darker by the second, but I can read his sneer. "Why don't you tell *me*? You're the one who's psychic."

"I don't know. It has something to do with that Monvor file."

"Gold star. Of course it does. Shay and Nate and Billy and their crowd — they were so cool. I just wanted to hang out with them. We went swimming, played softball, I sneaked them into the country club. . . . They liked me! And I agreed with what they were doing, too. I mean, what Monvor was doing was destroying real estate values. Of course my dad couldn't see that. He was too busy selling houses to the executives."

He pronounces the word *ex-EC-yoo-tives* in a deep, prissy voice, just like Franklin Ferris would. *He hates his father,* I realize. He had vandalized his own office. That peanut butter on his father's desk was *personal.*

"I wanted to help them. Why not? So in August, when they were getting set to maybe leave, I told Billy I could find him evidence. And I broke into Hank's house. I knew his code — he told me it was the day he met his fiancée, and I knew it, I was there at that party, I remembered. I got Nate into that party. That's where he met Hank. Hank hardly noticed us, so when he told me how he picked his code, he had no idea I knew it was July fourteenth. It was so easy."

"So you were friends with Nate and Billy."

"I was friends with all of them! Now Shay treats me like I'm only the person who sold her the house. She forgets." Jeff scowls.

"So what happened next?" I ask.

"I thought I did a great thing. Look at what Monvor was doing back then — destroying the land, lying about it — they deserved it. And Hank Hobbs deserved it, too. What a snob. He looked down on my dad and me, treated us like rubes who didn't know anything. He didn't care about Beewick. He'd just work here and use it for what he could, then move on to somewhere else."

"But what happened, Jeff?" I ask. "After you stole the file and gave it to Billy?"

"My dad guessed who stole it," Jeff said. His mouth became a thin line. "He told me I was stupid. That I couldn't alienate Monvor, it was half our business — what if they found out? He practically kicked me down the stairs. He said" — and again, Jeff uses that same deep, caricature of a voice — "'Get it back, boy! Or I'll turn you in myself, and you'll go to jail!' So I went back to Billy and said, hey, sorry, I need it back. And he said no."

"And that made you mad."

"No, I expected that. So I offered him money. Some of the money I'd saved for college, because my old man didn't believe in college — it's like, you need a diploma to sell houses? — and Billy just laughed at me. He said, 'Who do you think I am? I'm not going to sell out my friends.'"

"So you found someone who would sell out his friends. Nate."

"Not only did he take the money, he negotiated a better price." Jeff laughs hollowly. "All my college money. And he uses it for the down payment. And he says to me, 'At least you'll make your commission, Jeff.' Ha. And I never did go to college, thank you very much."

"And Billy suspected."

"Yeah. He didn't know who sold him out, but he called me, threatened to go to the papers, tell them what was in the file and let the chips fall. Well, I couldn't let that happen. I told him to meet me at the house. I knew it would be empty. I still had the keys, and Shay hadn't changed the locks yet. So we talked, and he made me so mad. I tried to explain about my father, about *jail,* and he told me I had no commitment, I was a hypocrite. 'You pretend to love this place and then the first chance you get, you sell out. . . .' And I hit him, and he came after me, so I hit him with a log from the fireplace, and he cracked his head on the mantel. Wow, he was tall. I still remember his head hitting — *crack* — and the way he went down. And the blood."

"You wrapped him in the shower curtain and dragged him out. And then you tore up the carpet. You pretended you did it as a favor." And Nate took the credit. He told Shay he'd done it. It was typical of him.

"It took me a long time to be able to sleep at night," Jeff said. His voice was close to a whine. "I'm not a monster."

"What happened with Hank Hobbs? Did he know you killed Billy?"

"He walks into the realty office twenty years later and doesn't remember me. But he's looking for a major property, so I show him the house I bought for an investment. He flips for it. Has to have it. Everything is going great, and then, that last day . . ." Jeff shakes his head. "I do such a stupid thing. We go out to the house together for a last walk-through, and my hands are full of papers and my briefcase and my cell, and so I say to him, just punch in my code, and I tell him the numbers, and he punches it in, and I see him looking at me, and I realize that he knows that I have the same code as he does, and how could that be?"

"But why would you use it, too, all those years later?"

"To remind myself of what I'm fighting for." Jeff's face is harsh. "I'm not content to be a townie.

I want to be bigger than that. Every single day I punch in my code, my password, I remember that I can do the hard stuff. I can win."

"What did he do?"

"Yeah, Hank. He's just looking at me, and I see that something clicks for him. Maybe he's already living in the past, seeing the girl again, that Betsy. I know he's thinking — *Here's the guy who broke into my house, all those years ago.* And I even see the moment when he makes the leap — *And what happened to that kid, that Billy Applegate? Could that be connected?* And meanwhile we're going through the house, talking about this and that, and I'm being totally cool, but I can read him like a book. So here's what I do. I think of the plan right on the spot. I say, 'Hey, you need to see the house from the water,' and he's not that interested, but I push it, in a nice way, and he says, 'Okay, yeah, we can go on my boat.' I manipulate him, see, so that he'd be hurting my feelings if he put me off. And then, once we're on the boat, the rest is easy."

The rest is easy? Murdering someone, watching them drown, that's easy?

"I know what you're thinking. You're disgusted, right? But listen to me, Hobbs wasn't a nice man. He cheated on his wife. He covered up what his company did, and then he tried to pay blood money to fix it, just because he wanted to retire here. And he tried to get your aunt fired, don't forget that!"

I feel the edge of my cell phone with my foot. I nudge it, trying to get it closer to the surface. I only succeed in pushing it deeper. But at least I know where it is.

"Yeah, old Hank wasn't a great loss to anyone. Whereas I'm a part of the island's history. I buy houses and renovate them. I run the annual Chamber of Commerce drive to help needy kids. I coach the high school swim team for free. . . ."

"The andro," I say. "That was yours."

"I only give them what they ask for," Jeff says. "You don't think the other kids are doing it, the kids from the rich communities on the mainland? Come on! And it's not a steroid, you know. It's a precursor. There's a difference." Jeff looks annoyed now. "You know, we're wasting time. It's dark now, I don't have to wait anymore. You can help me load Billy onto the sled."

"No."

"It's not far. I pulled up real close. I have a four-wheel drive."

"I'm not helping you."

Jeff laughs. "What, you think you have a choice?"

I can't feel the cell phone with my foot anymore. It doesn't matter — he'd never give me a chance to call anyone. But I've noticed something else. He's dropped his hand, the one holding the coiled rope. The rope has uncoiled, and his foot is tangled in it.

"Okay," he says, handing over the shovel. "You dig, I'll haul."

He's not kidding. I am not the strongest person. But I have my surprise on my side and, if I'm lucky, a certain lack of balance going on with him.

I grab the shovel and push it right back at him, hard, in the stomach. He is surprised. It wouldn't work, except he has to step back, and his foot gets caught in the rope. I give the shovel another push, and he goes over.

TWENTY-NINE

Now the nightmare is real. Crashing through the underbrush in a blind panic, not remembering where the trail is, the swamp sucking at me like a breathing monster, trying to bring me down. He's behind me, panting, not yelling, just running, and I know my head start is going to dissolve.

The cover of the trees helps. He can't see me. I run as quietly as I can, but it's hard not to make noise in a swamp. Things snap and rustle, and I hear him change direction and come after me again.

I burst through a thicket. Brambles tear at my skin. I push through, fall, get up, run around a tree, and almost bump into Nate.

He jumps and catches me. "What are you doing?" he practically shouts.

"Shhh!" I start to sob.

"Gracie, what's going on? I followed you from the ferry, and let Shay know. I just want to talk to you, I've been looking . . ."

"Let her go, Nate."

Jeff stands with the shovel. Casually. Dead-eyed.

"What are you talking about, Jeff? Gracie . . ."

"I know about you," Jeff says. "When you

reappeared on the island, I looked you up. Your life played out just the way I thought it would."

"He killed Billy," I tell my father. "And Hank Hobbs."

"You killed Billy? What? Why? You hardly knew him!"

"Didn't you suspect it?" Jeff asks. "Come on, Nate. Did you really think he just disappeared?"

"Yes!"

"I don't believe you. You knew I did it and you walked away, with money in your pocket and the girl, right? You know what it looks like? It looks like you were an accessory. I can say you even helped me hide the body, and who's going to doubt me?"

"What do you want, Jeff?" Nate asks. I hear him swallow. He's just beginning to understand what he's walked in on.

"I want you to let her go and walk away. Find another one of your identities and get lost. Get lost for good."

"She's my daughter."

"Yeah, that meant so much to you."

I feel Nate's fingers loosen on my arm. Feel his muscles relax.

And then a strange thing happens, stranger than maybe anything that's ever happened to me, and that's saying a lot. I know what he's going to do before he does it. And it isn't because I sense it, it isn't a psychic thing. It's a connection. One I didn't even realize we had.

So I move when he moves. I bend my knees just as he pushes me down. I tuck and roll as he catapults forward and slams Jeff Ferris with a fist on the side of the head, a blow I can hear, knuckles against skull, and then kicks him somewhere in his midsection and pushes him down.

But Jeff grabs his legs and yanks, and Nate topples. They grapple in the mud. I hear the blows and hear my father grunt.

I crawl toward the shovel. I stand, but I'm weaving, and I can't get a good shot at Jeff. I can't imagine I can slow him down. They are charged with adrenaline, and I see Jeff's fingers tighten on Nate's throat.

I feel a hand on my shoulder. I haven't even heard him come up.

"No need for that, Gracie." Joe's voice is calm. It's easier to be calm when you're holding a gun. "Jeff, get up. It's over."

THIRTY

I meet Nate at the inn, where he's spent the night. He and I had stayed over an hour at the police station last night, talking about what happened. In another room, Jeff Ferris had confessed to everything he'd done.

The venom of years had spilled out. How he had done so much for the island, and no one appreciated it. How he knew Mason and his friends had vandalized his house, so he got back at them by framing Mason for breaking into my house, and maybe for the Hobbs murder. He even trashed his own office so Joe would think the kids did it.

And his envy spilled out, too. How much he hated Hank Hobbs, who could so easily buy the house Jeff had bought but couldn't afford to live in.

His father refused to hire a lawyer for him. Jeff was on his own.

And Joe had suspected Jeff from the beginning. He'd been quietly gathering evidence while I was running around trying to pin it on everybody else.

Now, Nate leans against his car. "I'm sorry I can't stay longer, but Rachel wants me home. She's so glad you're okay."

"You're not going to Russia, are you?" I say. "You're leaving again."

He shakes his head. "I know you see things. Don't *imagine* them, too."

I fix him with my gaze. I pin him down. "Tell me the truth, for once."

He looks away, then looks back again. "Well," he says, "I guess I am leaving her, then."

"You're a real piece of work, Dad," I say.

His mouth twists in a way I haven't seen. "Yeah. I really thought I was ready to stick this time. Look, Gracie, everything you think about me is probably true. I've bounced from family to family. I don't mean to leave. But I do."

"It's just so weird and awful, having brothers and sisters I don't even know about."

He looks startled. "What brothers and sisters?"

"The kids in Tampa — Bunny and Ben."

"How do you know about Bunny and Ben? Okay, never mind. They weren't mine. I was married for less than a year. They were my stepkids. I'm a deadbeat dad on a technicality. I didn't owe Leslie child support. I mean, except in her own mind."

"What about Cheryl Ann? You stole her money and her wedding album?"

"Her wedding album?" He laughs. "I'm sorry, it's just that . . . I didn't take her wedding album. We weren't even married. We only had a 'commitment ceremony' — her idea, I assure you. That

album is probably kicking around the house, I bet —
the house was always a mess. I might have lifted a
few bucks when I left, though."

"Like you'll do with Rachel."

"Serves me right, I guess," he says. "I came here
so you *wouldn't* find out these things. When Shay
sent that private eye after me, I was afraid of what
he'd dig up. So I came here to talk to her, to see you.
I'm glad I came, even though now you know what
a crook your old man is."

"You're not just a crook, you're a sociopath. I
don't know if anything you told me is true."

"Well, now is your chance to ask."

"Did you suspect that Jeff killed Billy
Applegate?"

"No," he says, shaking his head. "I never
dreamed that Billy was murdered. Of course I
didn't think Jeff killed him."

"Did you really think you were manic-
depressive? Is that really why you left?"

He hesitates. "No."

I think back to the way he told the story, how
sincere he was, how, even though I was resisting
him, I was listening the whole time. The hurt of it
takes my breath away. What a good liar he is.

"You're sure good at telling stories," I say. I hear
the bitterness in my voice. "It's a wonder you're not
a millionaire."

He steps toward me and curves his whole body

toward me, lowering his head so that he can speak softly. "I wasn't afraid of losing my mind. But the rest of it is true. I did think I was hurting you. I know I was hurting your mom. I wasn't cut out for marriage."

"Did your father really commit suicide?"

"Yes."

"He had cancer! You're still lying!"

"And he took his own life when it got really bad."

"Oh." Suddenly, I feel deflated. I realize that the facts don't really matter. He lied to me once, and now I'll never quite believe him, even at his most sincere. "So why did you ask me to come back to Rachel's, then?" I ask. "You knew you were going to leave her."

"I was trying to stay," he says. "I always want to stay, kiddo."

"You know, I thought it might have started here, when you took the bribe and betrayed your friends. But it probably started way before that, didn't it? People don't matter to you. Nothing matters to you. I bet you gave away your *dog* when you were little."

"How'd you know?" He grins, but I don't smile.

But suddenly, to my surprise, his face changes and he steps forward and hugs me, really hugs me. He lifts me off my feet.

"This matters to me," he says in my ear. "This is the one true thing I know."

For a moment, I just sink into it. The feeling of being loved.

He pulls away. His hands dangle by his sides now.

"If you love me, then try," I urge him. "Try with Rachel. Get the baby. Start again. Do it right this time."

"Oh, Gracie. I don't think I can. She expects too much of me."

"Well, I do, too, and you love me," I say. "You've got a two-hour trip to consider your options. I'll call at eleven A.M. and if you're not there, I'll put Joe Fusilli on your tail."

"You'd do that to me?"

"In a heartbeat."

He cocks his head and looks at me. "You know, sweetie, that you can't make someone stick. You just can't. No matter what you hold over their head."

He's right, of course. I can't reform him.

"Just go with her, then. Help her get Sonia. Don't take that away from her, too. You can leave later."

"I'm afraid the die might be cast."

"You mean the money? For the rent and the airline tickets and things?"

He shakes his head in a marveling way. "You know that, too?" He sighs and gets in the car. "I guess I've got some thinking to do. I'll be in touch."

I watch him drive away. I don't know where

he's going. I think he'll go back to Rachel, just because he doesn't want Joe Fusilli on his trail. But I really don't know.

I stand there, watching, until I can't see his car anymore. I feel so tired. Tired of looking at all the cracks in love, all the imperfections. Tired of him. I don't want him in my life.

But there he is.

THIRTY-ONE

When I turn, Shay is waiting. She is always waiting. She waited for me to grieve for my mom. She waited for me to accept her. She waited for me to love her. She'll never stop waiting.

"Can I buy you breakfast?" she asks.

We start walking toward the diner.

"He's a real creep," I say.

"Yeah," she says. She hands me a tissue, and I wipe my tears.

"Did you make up with Joe yet?"

She stretches her arms above her head and smiles. "Not yet. But I feel a thaw coming."

We walk up the hill silently for a minute. "I thought you weren't coming back," Shay says. "I was so scared you weren't coming back."

"I want this to feel like home," I say. I want to be honest with her. "And sometimes it does. But in a way, I'm still looking for whatever that is."

She lets out a breath. "Okay."

"And I can't get over that you lied to me."

She stops and faces me. Her hair blows crazily in her face, the way it does. She's not wearing makeup, and everything looks naked on her face, all her emotion, all her feeling.

"Well, you're just going to have to get over it," she says.

I laugh at her fierceness. I can't help it.

"And stop saying that I lied," she goes on. "You know darn well what the circumstances were. You can't expect to know every detail of my past."

"Did you ever have a crush on Nate?"

She's startled. "Nate? No. I left that to Carrie."

"Did you like him?"

"Sure. Everyone liked Nate. But I guess maybe there was something about him I didn't trust . . . some instinct, because when Carrie fell for him, I was worried. Something . . . something seemed to be missing in him. But she loved him, so there was nothing more to say."

"You didn't go to the wedding."

"I was in Spain."

Shay opens the door to the diner. She smiles at Josie, the waitress, and holds up a finger, which means this morning she wants coffee. I know her routine as well as Josie does.

"Tea, Gracie?" Josie calls.

I nod.

Shay slides into a booth. Josie brings the coffee, and Shay takes the first sip with great appreciation, sniffing it first, curling her fingers around the thick mug. She smiles her thanks at Josie, asks her how her son is doing.

I am beginning to realize, as Zed told me, how lucky I am. And if making this work takes work, I'll work it.

"I don't expect to know everything," I say to her. "Just the important things. It's just that . . . there were secrets in my family. Things my mom couldn't tell me. And my dad is obviously one major liar. So I think I'm making a decision in my life to live differently. And I'd like it to start with you."

"Fair enough." Shay puts down her mug. "Fire away."

"Who was Diego's father?"

Shay takes a sharp breath. "Well, you certainly cut to the chase."

She doesn't want to do this. I see that. I see something there so deep, it hurts just to probe it.

She takes a sip of coffee and nods again.

"His name was Pablo," she says, and our long morning together begins.

About the Author

JUDE WATSON is the best-selling author of the Jedi Apprentice and Jedi Quest series. She used to live in the Pacific Northwest and now lives on the East Coast. This is her second Premonitions mystery.

Who says reading is boring?

Summer Boys

Sunscreen doesn't keep you from getting burned by hot boys.

6X

the uncensored confessions

Your backstage pass on the road to fame.

South Beach

Hot sand. Hot clubs. Hot guys.
What more could two girls want?
Try the same boy.